Also By Rebecca Massek

The Bell Tower Series

Slowly & Surely: A Bell Tower Novel

Utterly & Madly: A Bell Tower Novel

Truly & Deeply

A Bell Tower Novel

Rebecca Massek

ISBN 13: 979-8-9924498-0-8

Cover design by: Rebecca Massek
Printed in the United States of America

To everyone who believed in my little book. And to everyone ready to trust again.

"There is no timestamp on trauma. There isn't a formula that you can insert yourself into to get from horror to healed. Be patient. Take up space. Let your journey be the balm."

Dawn Serra

Content Warning

There are several topics covered that might be triggering to some readers. Please review this list and make an informed decision whether to continue reading.

Domestic Abuse

Torture

Hospitalization from assault

Allusions to non-consensual sexual activity

Parental abandonment & death of a parent

Prologue

Addy

Shards of glass ripped my skin. Blood trickled down my scalp, dripping from my hair. I couldn't breathe, couldn't think.

The heavy thud of boots treading on hardwood echoed in my ears. I could feel fingernails digging into my skin.

The sharp pain of my ribs breaking forced my eyes open.

I was breathing heavily, but I wasn't there. I wasn't in that room. I wasn't covered in broken glass. It wasn't *his* shoes crunching.

I was on the trail.

I was running.

The blood was sweat.

The boots were my sneakers on the hard dirt.

The sharp pain in my side was a stitch from pushing myself the last mile on no sleep and no energy.

I stumbled to a stop and my hands landed on my knees. I couldn't breathe. Every time I tried to inhale it stopped in my throat. I couldn't get any air into my lungs and they screamed at me.

Fuck.

I closed my eyes and forced myself to take three deep breaths through my nose. In for four counts, hold for four counts, out for four counts.

Flashes of red and blue lights flickered behind my eyes. I opened them and stared up at the sky. It was bright blue and clear. I focused on my senses.

I could hear the birds in the trees. The wind cooled the sweat on my face. My leggings were soft and smooth under my hands.

I was fine. I was alive. I was healthy.

***

"Another bar fight?" Dr. Laura, my therapist, looked at me over the top of her cat-eye glasses.

I sighed and fiddled with the chain of my necklace. An old nervous habit.

"I wouldn't necessarily call it a fight."

"Tell me what happened," Laura was always patient, never judgmental. No, my judgement always came from myself and my questionable decision-making skills.

"Raelynn saved me from a terrible date with a guy I'd met on a dating app. I hadn't even wanted to go on them, the apps, but *someone*," I gave Laura a pointed look, "insisted I start pushing myself again.

"He was disgusting – unwashed, rude, and more interested in the game on his phone than me. She called me to get me out of it, and then we went to a bar – the one that just opened up on Smith. Everything was going great. I was chatting with Raelynn, my panic was at a minimum. I was fine. Until this guy walked up from behind me and grabbed my arm."

2

I closed my eyes at the memory of the fear and panic that had flooded my system over one simple touch.

"I overreacted. I know that now, but in that moment, I was so scared. I elbowed him, and he fell backwards over a table. He bruised his ego more than anything, but he still made a huge scene, and the bartender had to call the police to get him to calm down.

"He ended up not pressing charges once we'd talked it out. He thought I was his friend, that's why he had grabbed me. I apologized for shoving him, and he was really quite gracious about the whole thing, in hindsight. It helped that the bartender saw everything and explained how it looked to the officers."

"It sounds like you were very lucky this time, Addy," Laura said, tapping her pen on her notepad. "You weren't so lucky last time when you spent the night in jail on assault charges. The only reason those were dropped was because of the security footage at the bar."

"I know," I grumbled.

"Tell me, what were you feeling before the incident?"

I paused and thought back. "I was uncomfortable from the bad date. I hadn't wanted to go in the first place, but Raelynn had insisted. She knew that you thought it would be good for me to get back out there, and she agreed. She wanted me to see that not all men are dirtbags. She wasn't right, of course, but the thought was nice. And then when we got into the bar I was on edge."

"That's not a feeling, Addy," Laura reminded me gently. We'd worked on this, on avoiding feeling my feelings by not giving them a name.

"Right," I sighed. "I was nervous. Anxious. Scared. I was jumping at every little noise and holding my breath the whole time we were in there. But it had been getting better, the longer we were there. I was less jumpy. I let my guard down, a bit."

"And when the man grabbed you?"

I closed my eyes and put myself back in the bar. The music had been loud and so had the chatter. Raelynn had been talking non-stop since we'd arrived, trying to distract me from my awful date. My drink was cold on my fingertips, and the whole place smelled like peanuts and pretzels. My heart had been hammering since we'd walked in and sweat beaded on the back of my neck. I was hyper aware of everything around me, every person that walked through the door. Then, Raelynn had touched my wrist to get my attention, and when I finally focused on her I'd felt the strong grip on my arm.

"Panic. Fear. And…"

Something red hot flickered in my stomach at the memory.

"Anger," I said, opening my eyes and looking at Laura. She had a soft smile, like she'd known what I was going to say and was happy I'd found the word. "I was angry?"

"Why do you say that like a question?"

"Because…" I sat back in the chair and ran my fingers down the chain of my necklace. "Because why would I be angry? I *get* scared and panicky, but angry doesn't make any sense to me."

Laura looked at me for a long moment, almost as if she were waiting for me to say something. But two could play that game. I simply watched her, waiting for her to help me through this. That was her job, after all. Finally, she sighed.

"When faced with dangerous situations, or situations that our brains deem dangerous, our bodies are conditioned to do one of three things: fight, flight, or freeze. Often, after traumatic events in our lives, our bodies can develop an exaggerated response to certain stressful situations. In your case, I think we can safely assume that any unwanted or aggressive physical contact would trigger a post-traumatic sympathetic response in your nervous system."

"And what does that mean in English?"

She smiled softly and leaned forward, resting her arms on her desk. "It means that when your body thinks it's in danger of being attacked again, it puts you right back in the moment of the triggering

4

event. In your case, Derek."

I flinched away from the name. "That still doesn't explain why I was angry."

"My guess would be that at the time of the inciting event you were probably feeling a multitude of things," she said calmly.

I nodded as it clicked into place. "Anger being a big one," I sighed. "I was angry then. Angry and scared for my life."

"And those emotions are imprinted on the fight or flight response of your nervous system."

I nodded again, looking down at my hands. It wasn't until a warm tear dropped onto them that I realized I was crying.

"What's going on in that head of yours, Addy?"

I took a deep, shuddering breath. "I don't want to be angry and afraid all the time. I don't want to knock someone over just because they touch me. I don't want to be so distrustful of everyone around me that I can't enjoy being out with my friends. I don't want to have panic attacks and flashbacks in the park and have people look at me like I'm crazy. I don't want to live like this anymore."

Laura's eyes were kind as she stood and made her way to kneel next to me. She placed a hand gently on mine and kept her gaze on me. I knew she'd never say it, but she was so happy to hear that. It had taken a year for me to admit that out loud.

"That's the perfect first step, Addy," she said kindly. "We'll keep working on it, and as long as you do the work, you'll get your life back. It's not going to be easy, but I know that you can do it."

I felt a small smile lift the corners of my mouth as tears ran down my face.

When I walked out of Laura's office that day, I knew that I wasn't cured. But I felt better than I had in a long, long time.

Chapter One

Addy

One Year Later

Nothing like some drunk asshat who won't take a hint after an already crappy day to make someone contemplate first degree murder.

All I had wanted to do was to sit alone at the bar and have a few drinks to take the edge off a hellish day, but no.

Raelynn couldn't understand why I chose to try to unwind at bars. I couldn't quite explain it. Maybe it was because I'd met *him* at a bar. I felt the need to reclaim them. Show the universe that I wasn't some scared victim.

I was stronger now than I had ever been. I still had a hoard of issues to work through, but my social anxiety was lessening each time I went out. So, I forced myself to keep going out.

Unfortunately, other people were often out too, and they had this nasty habit of ruining what little peace I was able to find.

"Hey sweetheart, can I buy you a drink?" Asshat slurred.

"No," was my only response.

"C'mon!" he jostled his way next to me. When he put his arm around my shoulder, I shrugged him off. "Bartender, two more of whatever the lady's having!"

"I don't want a drink from you," I growled through my teeth. When he tried to touch me again, I stood and moved to the other end of the bar, taking my current drink with me.

"Baby, don't be like that!" he hollered, following me.

My teeth were grinding together so hard I thought they might break.

"You need to relax," he grinned sloppily as he grabbed my shoulder.

I was now past angry.

"What the fuck do you think I'm trying to do?" I snapped, twisting my body away from him and glaring into his face. "I was trying to relax and enjoy my drink when you so rudely interrupted me. What part of 'No' didn't you understand?"

"Look, I was just trying to be nice, you fucking hag," he spit. "I was only hitting on you out of pity, anyways."

"Well, lucky for you I don't want your pity, I want you to leave me the fuck alone," I huffed.

I turned away, thinking we were done. I'd been perfectly clear. He must've gotten the message by now.

"I don't want to leave you alone, sweet cheeks." His voice was right by my ear.

I turned quickly, making sure I didn't touch him, and stared at him.

"You know who I feel really sorry for?" I asked, my voice pitched so that all of his friends at the table across the bar could hear.

"Who, baby?" He grinned, thinking he'd won me over.

"I feel sorry for your hand. It's got to be such an horrific experience to have to touch your dick every night in a desperate attempt to get you to shut the fuck up."

I saw his face fall, and then scrunch in confusion as he tried to determine whether he'd been insulted or not. Then his friends started howling with laughter and he realized that yes, that had in fact been an insult.

I smirked and turned back to the bar, certain he'd leave me alone now.

As I was turning, I felt a vice-like grip on my wrist, and was suddenly spun around and pinned against the bar. The lip of the wood dug into my back and I knew there'd be a bruise tomorrow.

My fists clenched and I was preparing to fight back when the man in the seat next to us slammed his glass down.

"I believe the lady said to back the fuck off," he drawled.

"Fuck you, dude, this is none of your business," Drunk Asswipe said, his grip tightening on my wrist.

I involuntarily flinched in pain. I was keeping my eyes trained on the guy who was holding me, waiting for the right opportunity to kick him in the balls.

My adrenaline was through the roof, and panic and fear were starting to tunnel my vision. This was how I ended up in trouble.

The man next to us silently stood up and turned to face us.

He towered over the guy holding me, and I watched as Drunk Guy's expression went from livid, to confused, to terrified.

He dropped my wrist like it was on fire, and quickly stumbled back to his table. I watched him go, my heartbeat pounding in my ears.

Unconsciously, I began rubbing my wrist to get some circulation back. When I was satisfied that Drunk Guy was no longer going to be a problem, I took three breaths. Just like Laura had taught me.

My vision came back, my pulse slowed, and I was able to talk myself down from the panic ledge more quickly than I'd ever done.

When I finally had myself back under control, I turned to thank the man next to me.

He was still standing, watching me closely, and when I looked into his face my breath stopped for a moment.

He was tall, obviously, but what hit me first was his physique. Under his T-shirt I could make out rippling muscles, barely contained by the fabric. His broad shoulders were hunched forward slightly.

I suspected that this was to make himself less threatening to me, and, given the circumstances, I appreciated that. His sharp jawline ascended into high cheekbones. His amber skin was flawlessly smooth and so tempting to touch. But it was his eyes that drew me in. They were unsettlingly deep and warm. They reminded me of hiding under the blankets as a child. Comforting, but also a little scary. Like he could know the secrets of my soul with one look. My heart rate kicked back up for an entirely different reason.

"Are you alright?" His voice swept through me like honey. It stuck on the inside of my ears, sweet and southern, with just a light drawl. It took me a moment to register that he was asking me a question which required a response.

"I'm fine," I shook my head to clear it, and noticed when his eyes dropped to my wrist.

"Did he hurt you?"

"Not seriously," I shrugged. "I've been through worse."

We looked at each other for a moment, heat flickering between us. I dropped my head when my mind started swimming and took a deep, steadying breath.

"Let me buy you a drink," I said. "To say thank you."

"It's really not necessary, I was just doing what anyone would have done," he said, his tone slightly embarrassed.

"Clearly not anyone." I gestured to the bar full of patrons who had not so much as glanced up at the commotion, let alone stepped in to help.

"If you don't want a drink that's fine, but I'm going to say thank you somehow," I continued. Our eyes caught and I suddenly realized how that had sounded.

I felt my cheeks heat and turned quickly to the bar, signaling to the bartender to get us more alcohol.

Because that's exactly what this situation needs, Addy, more alcohol, I chided myself.

When the drinks came we clinked our glasses together, and I saw the hint of a smile on his full lips as he sipped.

He looked at me for a moment before cocking his head.

"Let me ask you something - ," he paused, as if realizing we hadn't introduced ourselves.

"Addy," I filled in.

"Addy." The way my name rolled off his lips shot through straight to my core. "I'm Bell."

"Bell." I tasted his name on my tongue and decided I liked it. "Isn't that the name of a princess?"

He smirked and his eyes sparkled. "Is Addy short for addition? Your parents fans of math?"

A laugh bubbled out of my throat. The first true laugh I'd had in a long time. It startled me and I cut it off before it turned into a full laugh.

There was an awkward beat as Bell watched me struggle with the feelings swirling in my body. I realized I was being weird. *Just act like a normal human being, for Pete's sake!*

"Addy is short for Adelaide. My parents were actually fans of Australia, apparently," I joked softly, trying to keep my voice light.

"Bell is a nickname," he admitted, a smile playing on the edge of his lips. He didn't mention my moment, just continued the conversation as if nothing had happened. I was grateful for that.

"Then what's your real name?"

"Privileged information," he countered.

I took a sip and let the alcohol steady me.

"Well, Privileged, it's nice to meet you," I raised my glass.

"Likewise." His eyes sparkled playfully as he tapped his glass to mine and we took another drink.

We sat in comfortable silence for a moment, and he simply watched me. Feeling his eyes on me set my skin on fire, and all I wanted to do was bask in his gaze.

I hadn't felt such instant chemistry with a man since... But I had to admit, it felt nice. To be flirted with in a way that made me not want to immediately run away. I wanted to revel in the moment, but then my nerves started to creep in, my past reminding me that I shouldn't trust this connection. Nothing good came from chemistry.

"You were going to ask me something," I reminded him, clearing my throat.

"Yes, you distracted me," he muttered under his breath, but I still heard and rolled my lips to hide my smile. "What was your plan? If I hadn't heroically stepped in? What were you going to do?"

I looked at him and took another drink. He waited patiently, his eyes never leaving my face.

I took a deep breath and let out a long exhale. No part of me wanted to admit what my plan had been. Not to this perfectly nice, attractive, attentive, sweet stranger who for some unknown reason wanted to talk to me. I knew it would scare him off. He'd become uncomfortable and it would be another person that my trauma responses had alienated.

His eyes were soft as they watched my face, his expression open and curious, but not pushy. I took a deep breath and reminded myself that being honest was the only way to truly connect with new people. Thanks, doc.

"I was going to jam my knee into his balls, and then uppercut his face with my elbow," I said, my tone somber.

I waited for his reaction, thinking it would be demeaning or patronizing, as most men were when they heard someone like me say something like that.

Surprisingly, Bell laughed. It was a deep belly laugh, full of warmth and light. When he looked at me again there were traces of admiration.

"Just like that?" He sounded surprised that I was so matter of fact.

"Well, there were things I had to take into consideration," I said, slightly defensive. "First of all, I wasn't going to touch him until after he touched me. That makes it self-defense. And secondly, I wouldn't have touched him at all if there weren't security cameras in the bar."

"You clocked the security cameras?" His mirth died a little and was replaced with honest curiosity.

"I verified with the bartender that they worked before I ordered my first drink," I said softly.

Most people thought I was paranoid, and maybe I was, but there were some things that I just couldn't risk.

Bell's face softened, and his shoulders dropped a bit. Again, I knew this was to make himself less imposing, less threatening. It was all for my benefit. And it made me melt.

"That's really something you think about?" he asked.

"Yeah," I shrugged, trying to be casual. "Without security cameras it becomes he said, she said. I've been on the receiving end of one too many, 'I was just trying to compliment her and the drunk bitch went crazy and attacked me' tantrums. Spending the night in jail on assault charges is not fun."

"You've been to jail over this?" His tone bordered on outrage.

Again, I shrugged. I wasn't sure why I was being *so* honest with

Bell. Something about him was compelling, making me want to confide in him. I shook my head a little and felt my lips tighten. I didn't want to burden this stranger with all of my crap. I'd said too much already.

"Wow, so you really did have the situation pretty well handled, then?" he said. His tone now was casual, and I guessed that he had picked up that I was uncomfortable talking about it.

Seriously, this guy was that hot *and* empathetic?

"But that doesn't change the fact that I'm very appreciative that you stepped in," my voice was husky and low, intimate. I was flirting without my logical brain's permission. I blushed and took another sip of my drink.

As I watched, his eyes dropped to my lips and a flash of something flew across his face. Something that sent an electric shock straight to the pit of my stomach. Fear, I realized, but tinged with heavy arousal. Something I hadn't felt in years.

Then his eyes found mine again and he simply watched me. I kept expecting him to break away, to drop his gaze. Many would have. The intimacy of prolonged eye contact was uncomfortable for most people. But then again, I had a feeling Bell wasn't most people.

I watched his face, trying to read his thoughts. I couldn't see anything, and that was frustrating. People were normally so easy to read, but not Bell. After another few moments, I couldn't stop myself.

"What are you thinking?" I said softly.

He blinked and cocked his head to one side. Then, a wicked smile split his face, and my heart stuttered in my chest.

He moved slowly, his massive arm reaching out, pulling my barstool closer to his, until my legs were nestled between his thick thighs. Watching for my reaction, waiting for me to say no, he lifted his hand and brushed my hair back from my neck.

"You really want to know what I'm thinking, Addy?" His voice was rough, and I thought I was going to combust right then.

"Honesty is really important to me," I managed to mumble.

His eyes danced, and he leaned into me, his lips at my ear.

"Well, honestly, I was thinking about how good you would look spread out on my bed," his breath was hot against my skin, and I suddenly forgot how to breathe.

I could feel every place our bodies made contact. My knees on his inner thighs, my hand on top of his leg, his fingers playing at the nape of my neck, his lips…his luscious, sinful lips, teasing the shell of my ear.

I should have been defensive. I was certainly nervous enough that my fight or flight should have kicked in. I should have been pushing him away, angry at his presumptuousness. Afraid of his close proximity.

Instead, it took everything I had not to jump him right there. The way that he went from attentively listening to my plan of attack to looking at me like I was his favorite dessert made me dizzy, but the buzzing in my brain was making the corner of my lips turn up and my heart stutter. His scent, something sharp and so distinctly masculine, flooded my nose.

I could feel the heat of his skin, and I was terrified. But not of him. Of what he was doing to me.

He pulled back a bit to look into my eyes, and a current of electricity passed between us.

I leaned in slightly, overwhelmed by his presence and his scent. His energy wrapped around me like a drug, making the rest of the world disappear.

Then my phone buzzed in my pocket, and my heart dropped.

He heard it too, and his lips quirked in a small smile.

"Do you need to get that?"

I narrowed my eyes as I pulled my phone out of my pocket. Raelynn. I'd texted her half an hour ago to come pick me up.

I held a finger up to Bell and accepted the call.

"Hey."

"Hey, sorry, I just got your text!" Raelynn said over the phone.

Bell's hand was tracing circles on my thigh, and my brain buzzed with static.

"No worries, I'm just at Dylan's and was wondering … if you could pick me up," I told her.

I contemplated not having her come, but I knew that if I didn't have someone dragging me out of this bar, I would be on my knees worshiping the god in front of me in ten minutes.

And it wasn't that I didn't want to do that. Trust me, that's *all* I wanted to be doing. But I'd promised myself that I wouldn't let myself get hurt again. And Bell could hurt me. Badly.

"I'll be there in five!" Raelynn chirped.

"See you soon," I whispered, ending the call.

Bell was watching me closely, his hand now resting comfortingly on my knee. His touch was no longer suggestive, but supportive. My fight or flight couldn't have kept up if it wanted to.

"Leaving so soon?" he smirked.

"Well, it is a school night, after all."

"Yes, we wouldn't want you falling asleep during class," he said softly. "That would definitely warrant a trip to the principal's office."

I got an image of myself in a short skirt and a button up top, bent over a desk being punished by Bell.

Oh, this man could ruin me. I hadn't had a thought that dirty since… ever, honestly. Despite the growing fear in my heart, I decided to play along for a bit. I was having fun, I had realized. And I argued to myself it was therapeutic.

"I've never been to the principal's office." I let my fingers trace their way up his thigh. "I'm a good girl."

"I bet you fucking are," he nearly growled as my hand stopped just short of his inseam. Even through his jeans, I could feel the heat coming off his body.

I needed to stop. Right now.

Instead, my face broke out in a slow smile, loving the reaction on his face as his eyes dropped to watch my mouth.

It had been years since someone had made me feel the way this man did. I studied his face as I lightly bit my bottom lip. His eyes went huge, his breathing spiked, his thigh tensed under my hand.

His eyes met mine and I saw pure desire there.

I'm not sure what he saw in mine, but his gaze softened. He lifted a hand and traced my cheek lightly with his knuckles.

"You know, I don't just talk a big game," he said softly. "But I also don't want to scare you away, Addy. I'd never do anything you didn't want me to."

A surprised huff escaped me, and I defensively leaned back, turning my attention to my drink. My defenses immediately rose, and I needed distance and distraction.

"What makes you think I scare that easily?"

He leaned back as well, but I could feel his stare on my face. "Just a feeling," he mumbled.

I glanced at him from the corner of my eye.

He was right, however loathe I was to admit that to him. As attracted to him as I was, he also terrified me. The last person I'd felt this attracted to was *him*, and that had been one mistake after another. The memory of my ex was a splash of ice water on my libido, and I frowned as I sucked back the last of my drink.

"I have trust issues," I said softly, slowly turning to watch Bell.

He lifted one shoulder. "Me too."

I smiled and shook my head, amazed at how easy conversation was with him. He kept up with my mercurial mood changes better than I did.

"Maybe we could be good for each other," he said. "You never know?"

I opened my mouth to respond, but just then my phone buzzed again.

I looked to see a text from Raelynn. She was there.

I sighed and glanced at Bell. I knew that I should go, but there was a strong part of me begging to stay and see how good Bell could be for me.

"I have to go," I said, my voice sadder than I wanted it to be.

He looked sad too but didn't try to stop me. Instead, he pulled out his wallet and stood, slipping his jacket over his shoulders.

"I'll walk you out," he said, putting some cash on the bar.

"You don't have to –"

"A lady never pays for her own drinks," he said, winking at me.

Then he put his wallet in his back pocket and placed his hand lightly on my upper back. It wasn't sexual or possessive. It was a safety net to guide me through the crowd, and when we reached the door, he opened it for me and his hand dropped back to his side.

"You're quite the gentleman, Bell," I smirked.

"Always, for a lovely lady such as yourself." He put a little more twang in his voice and the way his eyes glinted mischievously made me laugh out loud.

We walked into the parking lot, and I immediately spotted Raelynn. I waved at her and then turned to say goodnight to Bell.

He was standing right behind me, so when I turned around he caught me off guard and I stumbled. His arms wrapped around me, steadying me and holding us close. I looked up into his face and saw that same something from earlier flash through his eyes. My hands were up against his chest, and I took the lapel of his jacket in my fingers.

"Thank you again, for everything tonight," I said quietly.

The way he was looking at me…the whole world faded away. I searched for the ever-present fear and anxiety that knotted my chest and found them mysteriously absent. The breeze floated around us, his scent fogging my brain and making my fingers curl into his jacket.

"Anytime, Addy," his voice was rough.

I bit my lip and then stood up on my tiptoes to place a soft kiss on his cheek.

His arms tightened around me, and my body pressed against his. I felt so safe. He looked at me seriously for a moment before leaning down slowly.

He paused just before his lips reached mine, a silent question hovering between us. I took a deep breath and, against my better judgment, nodded once.

His lips met mine, and the night sky exploded.

Lights went off behind my eyes as he kissed me. It was soft at first, but then a chemical reaction hit, and we both became desperate. His tongue lightly traced my lips, asking for them to open, and when they did, he claimed me. I felt his hand tangled in my hair, and I knew my arms were wound tightly around his neck, but the kiss was where all of my focus was. It was like breathing after being underwater.

Finally, he pulled away, and my body swayed to stay close to his. He chuckled, and my feet landed back on Earth.

I looked at him for another moment, memorizing his face. Knowing that I would probably never see him again.

Raelynn honked and it startled me out of my post-kiss high.

"Goodnight, Addy," he murmured, pulling himself away from

me and stuffing his hands in his pockets.

"Goodbye, Bell."

I nearly ran to the car and threw myself inside.

Raelynn's shit-eating grin told me she'd seen everything, and I was going to have to spill.

"Would you just drive, perv?" I snapped, but there was no bite to it.

I couldn't look out the window because I knew he was still standing there, and I knew from the heat of his gaze that he was watching me. I didn't want to see him looking after me, because I would never see Bell again. And I shouldn't have been so upset about that.

Chapter Two

Addy

"So, what the fuck was that, Addy?" Raelynn asked as soon as we were out of the parking lot.

"Long story," I sighed.

"It looked like it could've been a longer one," she giggled. "Why did you call me to come pick you up? He was delicious!"

"You know I wasn't going to go home with him," I said, exasperated. How quickly she forgot. "I promised myself that I wasn't going to have sex with anybody until I was in love again, and that right there was classic lust. Not love."

"What it was, was super fucking hot. God, I bet he's huge," Raelynn said in a far-off voice.

"What's Johnny doing tonight?" I asked, a casual reminder of her fiancée.

She smirked at me. "I can still ogle other god-like men, Adelaide. I'm engaged, not a nun."

We fell into the kind of silence that comes from years together. Raelynn was my best friend in the entire world.

We'd met the first day of freshman year in high school. Health class. Making fun of the teacher's horrible combover in the back row quickly grew into spending all of our time together. We'd been there for each other through every major life event since then. First cars, first dances, first times with boys.

She was the first person to get to the hospital after the attack, and she hadn't left my side until the restraining order was processed. She wasn't a big person, but her fiery personality filled every room she entered. We knew each other better than anyone else.

As we sat there, the town passing by out the windows, I knew she wanted to know more about Bell, and she knew I'd tell her when I was ready. I should tell her, but I could also guess what her reaction would be.

I sighed. There was no getting around it. She needed to know.

"He scared off some drunk douchebag who grabbed me," I finally admitted.

She immediately sobered. "Someone grabbed you in that bar?"

I nodded, waiting for the explosion.

"What the fuck?" she screeched, her eyes growing two sizes as she concentrated on not crashing the car. "Let me turn around and beat their ass! Why do guys think it's okay to just grab women in public spaces? Are you going to press charges?"

"No, there's no point," I shrugged. "It was just a little wrist grab. I would've been fine either way, but Bell intimidated the guy into backing off. So, I bought him a drink to say thank you."

After a moment of processing, Raelynn's eyes went back to their normal size. She looked thoughtfully out the windshield and then smirked at me.

"I bet there were other ways you could've said thank you."

"Probably," I admitted, a grin stealing its way onto my face. "He was gorgeous, wasn't he?"

"Out of this world," Raelynn agreed. "But you're not going to see him again, are you?"

I took a deep breath and looked out the window at the town passing by us.

"I'm too damaged, Lynnie," I sighed. "I wouldn't wish that on anyone, but especially not someone as kind as Bell."

The car was silent for a moment as my statement hung heavy in the air.

Finally, with no hesitation, "You know you're allowed to be loved, right Addy? You deserve someone who will protect you and love you and be kind to you. You're not a burden, and your past is not a non-starter. Not to the right person."

I stared resolutely out the window, her words scraping like nails on a chalkboard in my soul.

"Thanks, Lynnie, I know."

She sighed and said to herself, "But you don't believe me."

I pretended like I didn't hear her, and we continued the drive in silence.

***

The clock in Laura's office was ticking louder than normal. She was waiting for me to start speaking, as she usually did when we started our sessions. Typically, I had a laundry list of items to go through with her. But today there was only one thing on my mind, and it was the last thing I wanted to talk about.

I looked up from my cuticles, which had been holding my attention, and found Laura's steady brown eyes watching me from behind her glasses.

She held my gaze and then arched an eyebrow.

I blew out a sigh.

"I met someone this week," I finally admitted.

Her second eyebrow raised to meet the first and she sat forward in her chair.

"A male someone?"

I nodded. She sat back, studying me for a moment.

"I'm sure you meet a lot of male someones during an average week," she said, her voice soft and casual.

That's one of the things that I loved about her. It had taken me a long time to learn her tells of what was important and what wasn't. The forced casual tone was a big one.

"What's so different about this one?" she asked.

"Who says he's different?" I bit back, my arms crossing over my chest.

She smiled kindly, a knowing glint in her eyes. "You wouldn't have brought him up if you didn't want to talk about him. And you didn't immediately start cursing him, so I'm thinking that you had a positive interaction?"

I shrugged. Laura simply watched me. She didn't say anything else. She knew me well enough by now to know that if I wanted to talk about something I would, but that it might take me a moment to warm up to it.

The ticking matched pace with my heartbeats, steadying me and providing a level of comfort.

I looked at her timidly.

"He didn't scare me."

That admission did, though.

"What did he make you feel, then?"

"Safe."

The word was out of my mouth before I even thought about it.

Laura blinked, as if that was the last answer she was expecting, and then excitement flashed across her face. She schooled her expression to one of polite professionalism and scratched a note on her pad.

"What about him made you feel safe?"

I took a breath and thought about that one.

"He defended me. When some guy was harassing me, grabbing me, he stood up to him and got him to back off. And then he was totally okay with leaving me alone, but I wanted to thank him. So I bought him a drink...well, he ended up paying for the drinks, but my intention was to buy him a drink. And he – he wasn't aggressive, in his body language or anything. He was really gentle. And kind."

"It sounds like he's a decent person," Laura said, her eyes sparkling.

"He's a good person," I said with more conviction than I'd meant. Laura's lips twitched and she scribbled again. "I just mean..."

Laura cocked her head, waiting for me to finish.

"I flirted with him," I muttered, heat flooding my cheeks.

"How did that feel?"

"It was... fun," I admitted with a small smile. "That's the first time I've flirted with anybody since... well, you know."

"You should say it," Laura's voice was gentle.

I took a breath and felt my shoulders square defensively.

"Since Derek."

The taste of bile filled my throat, but I swallowed past it.

It was getting less painful to say his name. It took away the power he had over me every time I talked about it, and Laura was always reminding me why acknowledging my trauma was important.

"Did he flirt back?" Laura's voice grounded me in the present, another wonderful skill of hers.

I smiled to myself remembering his breath on my neck and his words that sent shivers down my back.

"Yes, he did."

"And how did your body respond to his advances?"

The smile slowly slipped from my face as I remembered. My heart had raced, but not out of fear. My breathing had spiked, but not in preparation for a fight. My limbs had tingled, and my skin had felt like it was on fire at his touch, but it only made me want him to touch me again.

"I let him touch me," I whispered in shock. "I let him get close to me, and I wasn't afraid."

"Addy," Laura's tone brought my eyes to hers, "that's amazing. That's a huge breakthrough for you. Some part of you trusted this man intrinsically. Instinctually. This is the first time you've told me about a man being close to you, flirting with you, touching you, and you not physically harming him, since Derek. Do you realize that?"

I nodded, unable to speak around the lump in my throat.

The room was quiet for a moment as Laura wrote something down and then simply looked at me.

I felt tears pricking the corners of my eyes. This *was* a big breakthrough for me. But I couldn't help but feel like I wasn't responsible for it.

Bell was. He'd made me feel safe. He made me let my guard down. I didn't choose to do either of those things, my body responded to him without my permission.

"So, are you going to see him again?" Laura finally asked.

"No," I croaked. "I didn't get his number."

"Why not?" Again, there was no judgment in Laura's voice, just simple curiosity.

I shook my head, wiping at the tears that refused to fall. "Because I'm scared."

"You said that he didn't scare you?"

"He doesn't," my voice was pleading with her to understand.

"He doesn't scare me, and that's terrifying. I have no control over my reaction to him. I don't want to trust him. I don't want to feel safe around him. I don't even know him. Why should some stranger make me feel better than I can make myself feel?"

"Addy," Laura started, her eyes trained on me and her voice steady, "you've done some incredible healing on your own. You've been dealing with your trauma. You've been working through your triggers. You have been brave and strong, and you've come such a long way since we first met. But there are some traumas that you don't have to heal from by yourself. Some that you can't."

"Isn't that what you're for?" I snapped.

She simply smiled and continued, moving past my outburst seamlessly. "You have trust issues, you know this. But how do you expect to work through those without at least trying to trust someone? You'll find that it's difficult to heal relationship traumas by yourself, because you won't be able to figure out what triggers you unless you're in a relationship."

I took a few deep breaths as her words sunk in and looked at her helplessly.

"So, what am I supposed to do?"

"I think the fact that you were able to be comfortable with this man –"

"Bell."

"Bell," she smiled. "The fact that you felt safe with him shows me that you're open to receiving positive male attention again. Now, I don't know if Bell is the answer. But I'd like you to at least consider being open to having a relationship with a kind man. It doesn't have to be romantic, it can be platonic, but a relationship where you work on trusting him. On being open and honest with him."

My heart stuttered in my chest as fear gripped me. I wanted to say no. But I'd been working so hard, facing so many fears, that I couldn't give up now.

"I guess all I can do is try."

***

"You have to come on this double date with me, Addy," Julia insisted as soon as I returned from my lunch break. "He only agreed to go with me if it was a double date. He's a little awkward, but I think he's so sweet. I know if I can get into conversation with him then he'll be more comfortable around me and –"

"You know that I don't do dates, Jules," I sighed, clocking in and turning my computer on. A barrage of emails greeted me, and I felt my head begin to throb.

Julia made her way out of her desk cubby over to mine. She had two manila folders in her hands, that way if our boss happened to look out of the big windows of her office she'd assume we were working on a project together.

"It's one date, and you'd really just be doing me a favor." Her brown eyes were big as she pleaded with me. "I'd owe you a huge one, and you could cash it in for whatever you wanted!"

I sighed and looked at her. If I was being honest, I didn't want to go on this double date because I couldn't stop thinking about Bell.

It had been over a week since we'd met, and he had consumed almost every waking thought. And more than a few non-waking ones. I shook my head. I was being ridiculous. Pining over a guy that I had talked to for not even an hour?

Anger and self-loathing bubbled in my stomach. I wasn't this type of girl. I had promised myself, after Derek, that I wouldn't fall for another guy until I knew him. Really knew him. And yet here I was, lost in daydreams about a demi-god with warm brown eyes and the sweetest smile.

"Fine," I snapped, more angry with myself than anything else. "I'll go on this double date with you." *Anything to get stupid Bell out of my head.*

Julia was stunned into silence for a moment, and then she squealed.

"Thank you so much, Addy, you won't regret it! And seriously, any favor you need, you just let me know."

"Can you take the Glickman account off my plate?" I responded immediately. Her face fell for a moment, but then she perked right back up.

"A fair trade if ever I've seen one," she chirped.

Instant regret kicked in. I did *not* want to go on a double date. But if it worked to get Bell out of my head then maybe it would be worth it.

***

I had never needed a run as much as I needed this one. My feet hit the gravel path, and I took a deep breath, letting the cool morning air wake my body up.

I hadn't slept well last night. I'd tossed and turned, regretting my stupid agreement to go on the double date with Jules.

Of course, Bell was littered there too. His strong arms. The way his body felt pressed against mine. The way he had claimed my mouth as his.

I could still feel his breath on my neck as he'd whispered, *"I was thinking how good you would look spread out on my bed."* Fuck, I felt myself tingle just thinking about it. And that was the problem.

Every night since I'd met him, I replayed our conversation in my head, and every night I touched myself, imagining it was his long fingers, his strong hands. I pictured his body poised above mine. I

28

heard his voice in my ear, I smelled his scent when I closed my eyes. It was bordering on obsessive.

And I didn't even know the guy! I was so frustrated. Sexually and mentally.

After Derek I had sworn off men. Not only because I was recovering in the hospital for a short period of time, but because I had jumped in headfirst.

We'd moved in together after a month of knowing each other. I was madly in love with him, and I didn't see the aggression until it was too late. He only put me in the hospital once. That was all it took for my world to shatter and for me to leave.

I'd signed up for self-defense classes, started doing MMA, and started running. Running was what got me through the darkest times. The times I wanted to just curl into a ball and fall asleep forever.

I had blamed myself for so long, and it took my therapist, my mom, and Raelynn a long time to get me to see that the problem was Derek. That it wasn't my fault.

I had finally accepted that, that him attacking me wasn't my fault. But I blamed myself for letting it get to that point in the first place.

That's when I decided that I wasn't going to get involved with someone again until I really knew them. Until I'd seen them at their worst and knew that I'd be safe. And most guys weren't ready for that. For my baggage, and everything that came with it.

In a way, I was grateful for Bell. He'd shown me that I could be attracted to someone again, which I hadn't thought would happen, honestly. And he had been very kind. I had noticed that he shrunk himself. To make me feel more comfortable around him. He was a big guy, and it was like he could sense that I might not feel completely safe around him. Yet, it was because he took that into consideration that I did feel safe with him. Safer than I'd felt with a man in a long time.

"But it doesn't matter, idiot, because you're never going to see him again," I huffed at myself.

I shook my head and pushed my feet deeper into the ground, kicking up my speed.

After I made it to the end of my six-mile loop and stopped at a bench to cool down, I noticed two guys who had been jogging behind me for about half a mile, also slowing down. I could feel their gaze on me, and I switched to stretching my arms.

I didn't have any music on my headphones, but I took them out anyway. My heart was already racing from the brutal pace I'd set myself, but now it was tinged with adrenaline.

I knew, instinctively, that they weren't dangerous, but I still didn't like the way they looked at me. I watched them from the corner of my eye as they kept coming closer, their eyes never leaving me as they smiled.

I ground my teeth and rolled my eyes. Could I just have some fucking peace, for once? Why was the entire male species hell-bent on ruining the things I liked the most. First my bar, now my run?

I shook my arms out and bounced a little on my toes, ready to take off again if they kept looking at me, when I heard a familiar voice call from behind me.

"Babe, there you are!"

I turned and saw Bell jogging lightly toward me. My eyes widened and my mouth dropped open a bit as I took him in.

His thick thighs were busting out of his jogging shorts, and he didn't have a shirt on. He was glistening with sweat, his pecs bouncing as he loped nearer. He had a large tattoo running down his left shoulder and over his chest, a lion piece it looked like, with lots of white ink that highlighted the details against his dark skin. His shorts left very little to the imagination, and I felt my mouth go dry as I dragged my eyes up to his face.

He was smirking. He'd seen me checking him out.

He stopped in front of me and reached out to touch my elbow lightly. His eyes flickered to the two guys that were now ten feet away.

I glanced back at them and saw them glaring at Bell.

I grinned widely as I realized he had yet again come to my rescue. Much less dire circumstances this time, but he was my rescuer, nevertheless.

"Have a good run, guys," I called out, slipping my hand into Bell's. For show, I told myself.

They began jogging and disappeared around the corner.

We watched them, and then turned back to each other, both of our eyes dancing. He lifted our hands and gently kissed the back of mine before letting it fall.

"I can't leave you alone for one second, can I?" he joked.

I shook my head, groaning. "I don't know what it is about the male species, but I'm starting to get pissed off."

"Well, you're hotter than the pavement in July, Addy," he said. His voice was casual, but I could feel him watching me. "It makes guys do stupid things."

I rolled my eyes and bent down to stretch out my hamstrings. I was *not* showing off my ass for him, I told myself sternly.

"Guys do stupid things regardless, that's not my fault," I said. "Besides, I highly doubt I really have that much of an effect on anyone."

"I wouldn't be so sure," he growled. I looked up, surprised at his tone, and watched his tongue dart out to wet his lips.

God, I'd been fantasizing about those lips. Mesmerized, I couldn't tear my gaze away. Then he was smiling that devilish smile and stepping forward a bit.

"I haven't been able to stop thinking about you," he said in a low voice.

I gulped and watched him.

"Your eyes, your smile, the way you felt in my arms," he spoke reverently, taking a step closer with each word until he was towering above me. And yet still I felt safe.

He brought his hand up and brushed his fingers along my cheek. He cupped my face in his hand and his thumb dusted over my lower lip, pulling it down slightly. I tried to resist the urge, but failed, and my tongue flicked out, barely brushing the pad of this thumb. His breath caught and his eyes flashed. I loved that I could do that to him.

A young couple with a stroller jogged by and we were brought harshly back to the reality that we were standing in a public park, not alone in a dimly lit bedroom. I stepped away from him and my fingers found their way to the chain of my necklace.

An awkward silence dropped between us, broken only by the slight breeze and the birdsong.

"Have you thought about me at all?" he asked, his voice suddenly hesitant.

As if I could lie. "A lot," I whispered.

A brilliant smile lit up his face and he laughed, carefree and loud.

"Thank god, I was worried I was going to look like a jackass for a second there."

I rolled my eyes and went back to stretching, but it was mostly for show. I couldn't shake my awareness of his body. He followed suit, his eyes still sparkling with delight.

"So, when can I take you out on a proper date?" he drawled.

I blinked, straightened, and stared at him. "I don't think that would be a good idea, Bell."

The words were out of my mouth before I could stop them. I could hear Laura's voice telling me it was time to give someone a chance, but I couldn't let that someone be Bell. I didn't want to ruin him with my baggage.

Bell looked at me, his eyebrows furrowed, and he put his hands on his hips.

As he did, I felt a flash of fear. Irrational, reactive fear. That fear made me take another step back, my shoulders tensing.

He blinked and looked down at his posture, and then he relaxed his pose and sat on the bench so that he was shorter than me. It was an inherently less threatening position, and I took a deep breath.

I had overreacted, but it had only proved my point to myself. I wasn't ready for someone as good as Bell. He would do something, I would overreact, and I'd ruin it.

"You don't want to go out with me?" he asked softly.

I sighed and ran a hand over the nape of my neck. How to explain?

"I don't think it would work, honestly," I said, my voice tender. "You're this incredible guy, and you're gorgeous, and kind, and selfless. And I'm..." I hesitated.

"We all have our baggage, Addy," he said, trying to keep his voice light. "I'm sure it's nothing we can't work through."

I half-shrugged. "Mine's a lot. It's not something I want to put on anyone, especially you."

"But –"

"It just... it won't work. I'm not looking to date right now, anyway."

It wasn't really a lie; I wasn't actually looking to date anyone. But with the way Bell made me feel, I knew that anything between us wouldn't be casual.

He looked at me for a moment, and I swear it was like my heart cracked in two. I hated to hurt him. But honestly, he couldn't feel the same way I was feeling. We'd only met once before.

"Can I give you my number anyway? Just... just in case you ever need a friend to talk to?" He was so hesitant. So sweet.

I hesitated a moment and then smiled at him. "Here," I handed him my phone.

We could be friends, if nothing else, right? Friends was harmless. Friends was safe. I knew somewhere in the back of my mind that I was lying to myself. "I'd like to be your friend, Bell."

His answering smile took my breath away. "Friends it is, then."

Chapter Three

Bell

It had been three days since I'd run into Addy at the park, and I still couldn't get the image of her wild brown hair catching the sunlight out of my head. My Pops would call me a lovestruck fool, and the thing that was scaring me was that he wouldn't have been wrong.

Addy mesmerized me.

The way her hair bounced when she talked. The way her eyes lit up when something challenged her. She was so serious that when she smiled it felt like a beautiful gift. It transformed her face, made her cheeks go rosy and her nose scrunch.

She was addicting, and all I wanted to do was spend every second of every day getting to know her.

And she scared the ever-lovin' hell out of me.

I had never met someone that took over my brain like she did. She took over other parts of me, too, but she'd insisted on us just being friends so I was trying to tame my baser urges.

I couldn't put my finger on it, but there was something about this woman that made me feel like she needed to be protected at all costs. And something else told me that she'd been the one protecting herself for too long.

I'd never felt the need to protect a woman before. My mom

leaving had caused some deep scars, and while my Pops had taught me to deeply respect women, I'd always figured they could take care of their own problems. I'd never gotten emotionally involved because I always knew it wouldn't last, and felt like they didn't need me.

I had never had a serious girlfriend. College was one-night stands or vacation flings that never lasted. When girls started to get too attached, I cut it off. I liked a good time, and hated hurting people, so it was easier to stop things before they ever got started.

It wasn't that I didn't trust women. It was more that I didn't trust myself. I was a dumbass who would fall head over heels for a girl if I wasn't careful. So I was always careful.

I'd never stood a chance with Addy.

I'd seen her in the bar, milking her drink, and hadn't been able to stop staring at her. She was so solemn. So tense. Her eyes were constantly darting around the room. As I'd watched her, she had rolled her shoulders and tried to relax, and then the tension would creep right back in. So she'd do it again.

It was like she was practicing. I'd been trying to get over my own stressful day, so I had been content to try not to creep too hard as I'd watched her. And she'd been making progress before that asshole had dropped in on her.

Then, as fate would have it, she escaped to me.

I would have been fine if she weren't feisty and flirty and clever and sad. She was so sad. I wondered if she even knew? Before I could stop it, my stupid heart had made a promise to try and make her happy. Against all odds and reason.

And then I'd tasted her, and the rest of me followed in my heart's footsteps.

Never before had I wanted to spend all of my time with a woman. I wanted to hold her in my arms and keep the world from hurting her. And I'd known her maybe a week. Shit.

"Yo, bossman," Greg snapped his fingers in front of my face.

I blinked back to reality. To the bar where I was unpacking glasses, frozen with one in midair as I'd thought of the little bombshell the universe had just dropped into my life.

"Sorry, man," I mumbled.

"You're not one to get distracted," Greg joked, his thick Alabama accent coming out as he poked fun.

I'd met Greg in college, and he'd been by my side ever since. The stereotypical Southern boy on the outside, but on the inside a quirky nerd with a heart of gold, Greg had been the one person in my life (other than my Pops) that kept me from losing my head. He was there through the dark years, and even now was keeping me grounded.

"Let me guess, it's that girl you met the other week?" His grin was still on his face, but it was being kept carefully in place.

He knew girls were a touchy subject, and he was always cautious when we spoke about them. Which was rare enough that we were rusty on our conversation skills.

I sighed and ran a hand over the back of my neck.

"Yeah," I admitted. "I ran into her the other day on my run."

"That's like…kismet," Greg said, arching a brow.

"It felt like it at the time, bud, it really did," I shook my head.

"What, she not interested or something?"

"That's the thing, I'm pretty sure she feels the same connection I do, but she insisted we stay friends." I continued unpacking the glasses so I didn't have to look at my friend as I admitted how much I hated that.

"And?"

"And what? She wants to be friends, so we're friends."

"Don't get all huffy with me, bucko," Greg shook a finger at me. "Have you reached out to her?"

"Well, no, I didn't want to overstep."

"I'd call her up and invite her out, as a friend, and get to know her better." Greg shrugged and took the now empty box from me. "If she wants to be friends, be friends. That's how my parents met, and they've been together forty years now."

"Really?" I leaned on the marble bar top and looked at him.

"Yep," Greg grinned. "My mom did the same thing to my Dad, told him she wanted to be friends first. He just kept taking her out, as a *friend*, and she eventually trusted him enough to fall for him."

"So, it was a trust issue?"

"Isn't it always, man?" He shook his head. "Nobody in this world isn't some kind of fucked up in the trust department, you and I included. I say, take her somewhere safe, with lots of people around, and do something friends would do. Something not too datey, and then see where it goes from there."

I felt my lips twitch into a small smile. "Anyone ever tell you you're a pain in the ass?"

He laughed. "Maybe, but I'm a genius pain in the ass."

***

My finger hovered over the call button. It'd been stuck there for five whole minutes as I waffled back and forth between texting her and calling her.

Greg and I had finished unpacking for the opening night of our new restaurant and brewery.

It'd been our dream since college. Greg was a brew master, creating unique flavor profiles that blew peoples' minds. I had always wanted to own a restaurant. Food was something that brought people together, made them happy. I wanted to put whatever happiness I could out into the world.

We figured, why not open a brewery together? We'd spent years doing market research, and looking for the space, and we'd finally found an old warehouse in the middle of downtown Hartworth. Justine, Greg's fiancée and our business manager, had helped with all of the minutiae of actually opening a profitable restaurant. We couldn't have done it without her.

Now, we were about two weeks from our soft open, and while Greg was nothing but excited, I was more nervous than a cat in a bathtub.

Suddenly, a pasty finger was pressing the call button on my phone. I looked up in panic into Greg's cocky face.

"Figured you needed a kick," he said, laughing.

I looked back at the phone just as I heard a faint, "Hello?" from the other end.

I cleared my throat and shoved the phone to my ear. "Um…hey there, how are you?"

Addy's voice was wary on the other end. "I'm fine? To what do I owe the pleasure?"

"I…" I glared at Greg's shit-eating grin. "I was wondering if you wanted to hang out?"

"Hang out?"

"Umm, yeah, but just as friends," I added hastily.

She was silent for a moment. "What did you have in mind?"

A breath of relief flooded through me. She wasn't immediately rejecting me. But now I had a new problem. I looked to Greg, who was having a conniption, he was so entertained.

"Zoo?" I said. I almost palmed my forehead. "Would you want to go to the zoo? There's an animal sanctuary about half an hour away from Hartworth that only takes in rescues."

She was quiet again, and I was sure I'd lost her this time.

"Sure, that sounds like it could be fun," she finally said.

A grin split my face. "Yeah?"

"Yeah." There was a laugh in her voice that I wanted to record to listen to over and over again. "When should we go?"

"How about Saturday? I can pick you up?"

"How about I meet you there." There was hesitation in her voice. Trust issues. Greg was an annoying fucker, but he wasn't usually wrong.

"Yeah, that's fine," I said. This was unfamiliar territory for me, but I wanted her to know she was calling the shots here. "How about we meet at eight? That'll give us plenty of time before it gets too hot."

She laughed again and warmth shot through me. "You're too right on that. Eight sounds great."

"Great," I smiled into my phone like a twelve-year-old. "It's called Graham's Animal Sanctuary, off of highway eighty-five."

"I'll see you there."

"See you then." I couldn't keep the smile off my face.

Neither of us immediately hung up. I wanted to keep talking to her. I should've hung up. Hell, I shouldn't have called at all.

"Bye, Bell," her voice was soft.

"Goodbye, Adelaide."

The line went dead and I blew out a breath I hadn't realized I was holding.

Greg poked his head up over the counter. I playfully took a swing at him and he ducked, laughing the whole time.

"That didn't sound so bad."

I sighed. "No, it went fine. We're hanging out on Saturday."

"So why do you look like you just ate the wrong end of a lemon?"

I rolled my eyes and leaned on the counter, dropping my head into my hands.

"I don't know how to be friends with a woman, man," I said, guilt washing through me.

Greg nodded knowingly. "Trust issues."

"Shut up," I grumbled.

"Hey man, I've known you for nine years and I've never once seen you with a long-term girlfriend. You have what can be categorized as 'flings' at best, and one night stands at worst," he shrugged nonchalantly, but his gaze was serious.

"I know, I've just never wanted that with someone. I've always been better off on my own."

"You also don't get hurt if you leave them first," he pointed out. "So tell me, why do you want to spend time with this girl so badly?"

I blinked. "I have no idea, man. She's just... different."

"Yeah, because she doesn't want to sleep with you," he mocked.

"It's not that. Well, not just that," I sighed.

I couldn't put my finger on why Addy was so different. She was unbelievably gorgeous, in a way that knocked you on your ass before you knew what hit you. But it wasn't that.

She just... she acted like she didn't need anyone. She was fiercely independent, and I'd never met a woman who was so insistent on taking on the world alone.

But at the same time, she gave her smiles freely, and she'd laughed at my jokes like we were old friends. And the way she'd kissed me, the way her body had melted into mine... it was archaic, but there was a part of me that wanted to show her that she could trust me.

Which was ridiculous, because I'd never done relationships before. I didn't have anything to offer. I didn't know how to love somebody. Greg had been right about my own trust issues. But something about Addy made me want to try.

***

Saturday came around quicker than I'd anticipated. There was so much to get done at the restaurant in the next two weeks that we were slammed. Trying to hire staff, set up the restaurant space, testing and refining the brews so we had booze to sell. It was all overwhelming.

Yet, every down moment of my day was spent thinking about Addy. The determination on her face when she'd confronted that guy in the bar. The daggers in her eyes when she'd waved off the joggers in the park. I thought about her eyes a lot.

The deep blue that turned stormy gray when she was angry...and aroused. The way her pupils had dilated when she'd watched me jog up to her. I'd felt her gaze on my body for days after.

And now I stood in front of my mirror, trying to figure out what was appropriate to wear on a friend date with a woman that I was desperate to taste again.

I finally settled on a linen button up and rolled the sleeves up to my elbows. My jeans were a bit tight, but I'd relished the way she'd watched my thighs and was hoping to tempt her just a little.

At a quarter to eight, I pulled into the parking lot of the zoo. As I approached the entrance, I bit back a groan when I saw Addy.

Her dark hair was pulled up into an untidy bun on top of her head, and tendrils of curls broke away and framed her face. She was wearing a light blue sundress that flared at her waist, showing off her curves. I had a semi just from the sight of her, and I had to actually take a moment to compose myself when she saw me and gave me a shy wave. I watched as her eyes swept over me, and I felt heat rising to my cheeks. Weird. I'd never felt self-conscious around women before, but Addy wasn't just any woman.

She was so fucking perfect.

"Hey, looks like I'm not the only one who likes to be early," she teased as I finally made it over to her.

"Better early than late," I joked back.

"This place actually seems pretty cool," she said, pointing to the bulletin board that had a piece on the foundation of the sanctuary.

"I used to come here all the time as a kid," I nodded.

We bought our tickets, each paying for our own (because we were just friends), and made our way inside.

Addy was entrancing. She wanted to stop and read every sign about every animal's story. She recited the fun facts for me like I couldn't read them myself, and I let her so I could hear her voice. She seemed like she was trying to keep her composure, but after a bit she was running from exhibit to exhibit, her excitement shining on her face. She was so free as she watched the animals with wide eyes. And then she'd look back at me and something would shutter behind her gaze. She'd straighten and run her palms down her skirt, like she was embarrassed.

I couldn't figure out why her guard was up. She kept at least three feet between us at all times, but I swear I saw her gravitate towards me. A few times when I caught her gaze, I watched her breath catch in her throat, and had to suppress my own desire. She didn't want to be friends, just like I didn't want to be friends.

But I didn't want to push her. I just wanted to be with her. Get to know her.

After a few hours of exploring every square inch of the sanctuary, we sat at the café, ice creams in hand.

Ice cream was a bad choice. I couldn't stop myself from watching the way her tongue curled around the spoon to get every last bit into her mouth, and I now had an uncomfortable situation that would require several minutes of breathing to fix before we could leave.

"So, who took you here when you were a kid?" she asked.

We hadn't said much about our personal lives, sticking to the safe topics like where the animals were from, so I was a little taken back at her question.

"My Pops," I said, a smile worming its way onto my face.

"That's nice," she grinned. I watched the sunlight catch a lock of her hair, turning it a warm reddish brown. "My parents were more museum people. It was very rare I got to see living things."

"Well, you looked like you were enjoying yourself," I smiled.

"I was," she admitted. "I am." She looked up at me from behind her thick eyelashes, her cheeks flushing pink. "I think we'll be really good friends, Bell."

Ice water would have been less jarring than that damned word. "Right, friends," I tried to keep my tone light. "Very good friends."

She must've heard something in my voice, because the wall was back up when I looked at her again. The same wall I'd seen as she'd walked to the car after our kiss. The wall that told me she wasn't expecting to see me ever again.

"Hey," I reached out to lightly touch her hand, and she pulled hers back. A sliver of fear ran across her face, which was quickly replaced by shame.

Oh…it finally clicked in my thick skull. She'd reacted the same way when my posture had gotten a bit too aggressive in the park. I'd clocked it, and backed off, but this moment cemented it.

Shit.

Anger flared through me. I wanted to kill whatever man made her jump like that. She'd talked about baggage. She'd told me her self-defense plan in the bar. I'd shrugged it off, knowing that women

44

had to be more on alert in this world, and hadn't thought anything of it.

Suddenly, her hesitancy made so much more sense. These were tricky waters to navigate, but something inside of me was screaming that I had to keep going. I had to make her smile. Make her happy. Keep her safe.

I looked at her again and lowered my head to catch her eyes.

"Hey," I said again, my voice softer. "I'm cool with being friends, Addy. I don't want you to think I'm not. I've got to be honest though, I've never been just friends with a woman, so you'll have to bear with me as I learn how, okay?"

Her eyes were pensive as she examined my face. I don't know what she saw there, but whatever it was I watched as a bit of the wall chipped away.

She reached across the small table and rested her fingers on the back of my hand. The simple touch sent fire across my body, but I didn't react. I waited for her to lead.

"Thank you for being so patient with me, Bell," her voice was soft. "I wasn't lying in the park...I have a lot of baggage. And I would feel horrible putting it all on you. That's why I want to be friends. It's just... easier. I promise."

"I promise, I'll be here for you no matter what you need from me," my voice was solemn. I'd never meant anything more than that statement. "I won't lie, I'm crazy into you, but I want you to trust me. So, friends it is."

She bit her lip and then nodded, a small smile lighting up her face.

I took a deep breath. Friends...right.

Chapter Four

Addy

Being friends with Bell was harder than I'd thought it would be. I kept telling myself to just leave him alone, that it would be easier if we just weren't in each other's lives. Then, he'd send me a text about a squirrel he'd seen in the park on his run, and before I knew it we'd be texting for hours. My brain didn't want to be his friend. My heart apparently had other plans.

A few days after our trip to the zoo, I felt my phone buzz in my pocket while I was wandering the candy aisle at the grocery store. I pulled it out and Bell's name lit up the screen.

"Hey there," I answered, tucking the phone between my chin and shoulder as I grabbed a box of chocolates from the shelf.

"What are you doing tonight?" His drawl never failed to make my heart sputter.

"Tonight?"

It was Monday night, and I'd had a hellishly long day at work, so my plan was to drink a bottle of wine by myself in my apartment and eat an entire box of shells and cheese before passing out. But I didn't think that was information Bell needed to know.

"Just hanging out in my apartment, why?"

"It's trivia night at my favorite bar, and I was wondering if you wanted to come? My friend Greg and his fiancée will be there, and our usual fourth backed out. What do you say?"

He sounded so hopeful, and even though I was exhausted I found myself saying, "That sounds fun! Tell me when and where and I'll be there."

He said he'd text me the details and as we hung up, I mentally kicked myself.

This was not the plan. The plan was to spend no more time with him and let this barely started friendship fizzle out on its own. Not meet his other friends and spend a Monday night on what was essentially a double date.

Then, the traitorous part of my brain that liked Bell more than I wanted to admit chimed in.

He was just inviting me out as a friend. His friends would be there, it was a public place, and they'd needed a fourth for their team. Nothing about this was a date. So, it was okay.

Even with that line of thinking playing in my head, I was mentally going through my clothes to put together a cute outfit.

***

The bar was full of trivia goers on a Monday night, so it was busy but not hectic.

I stood inside the doorway, scanning the room for Bell's hulking figure. I finally found it at a table on the other side of the room. My heart did a traitorous flip when it recognized him. He was dressed smartly, in slacks and a button up that was tucked in, leaving nothing to the imagination yet maintaining an air of professionalism.

Next to Bell was a shorter guy with messy, straw-colored hair and a big grin. He was cute, in a down-home American boy, kind of way. He had his arm around a tall, gorgeous woman who was laughing at something he'd said. The blond was dressed casually, jeans and a t-shirt, but the woman was in the remains of a business suit, her jacket draped over the back of her chair. Her curly hair was cropped close to her head and I was blown away by how stunning she was.

Bell looked up and caught my eye, waving me over.

"Guys, this is Addy, my new friend," he said as I sat down. "Addy, this is Greg and his fiancée Justine."

"Nice to meet you," I said softly.

"Nice to finally meet you," Greg had a Southern accent so thick that it was difficult for me to fully comprehend what he'd said at first.

My face must have given me away, because the table burst out in a fresh round of laughter.

"Don't worry, Addy," Justine said, her voice sharp with an Atlantic twinge, "you'll learn how to interpret Greg with time. The first time I heard him speak I thought he was trying to communicate with an animal."

That startled a laugh out of me. Greg's eyes twinkled as he stuck his tongue out at Justine, and then they shared a sweet kiss.

I turned to Bell and gave him a soft smile. "Are they always like that?"

"Absolutely," he grinned down at me. "You'd never know it, but these two were mortal enemies once upon a time."

"I'd love to hear that story," I chuckled.

"Later," Bell winked at me as the MC started the night.

It turned out that Bell was freakishly knowledgeable on a variety of topics. I kept waiting for a subject that he wouldn't be able to guess the answer to, but it never seemed to come. Sports, astronomy, earth science, pop culture, Bell seemed to know it all.

48

Greg and Justine were pretty good too, but by the end of the first round Bell had scored most of our points.

We went to the bar to get drinks for the table during the break and I told him how impressive his brains were.

He shrugged one shoulder. "I did a lot of reading as a kid, and things just stick in my head."

"Is there anything you don't know?" I teased, leaning against the bar.

"There's lots I don't know," he said. There was a smile on his face, but his tone had dropped to something more serious.

Our eyes held for a moment, and I knew the conversation could head in two directions.

One, I would ask him what he meant, and he'd tell me some deep truth about himself that would make him vulnerable and in turn I'd feel like I had to reveal something about me.

Two, I would turn to the bar and wonder where our drinks were, effectively ending the conversation.

I went with option two.

As I searched for the bartender I could feel Bell's gaze on my face, but he didn't push me. Instead, he waved a hand and the bartender magically appeared with the drinks for our table.

As we arrived back, we walked into the middle of a heated debate between Greg and Justine on the pros and cons of online dating. I tried not to flinch thinking about my last online date and instead settled into my chair and took a healthy swig of my drink.

"How in the world did y'all even get on this topic of conversation?" Bell laughed as he set their drinks down.

"Clearly that couple in the corner is on a first date," Justine said, pointing to a painfully awkward couple on the other side of the bar. "We were wondering whether they were on a blind date or if it was an internet date, thus the debate."

I observed them for a moment and then took another sip. "Definitely a blind date."

"What makes you say that?" Greg asked.

"It's too awkward not to be," I laughed. "Even with an internet date, usually you've at least talked to the person before. Nobody is that awkward with someone unless they've literally never met them before in their life."

"Maybe they just don't have any chemistry?" Bell offered, his eyes watching me carefully.

"Maybe," I said noncommittally. "But chemistry isn't everything."

"But it helps a lot," Justine wagged her eyebrows suggestively.

"Sometimes it doesn't," I muttered, flashes of red and blue lights playing through my mind.

Bell cocked his head and was about to say something when the MC started back up. His gaze lingered on my face, but I steadfastly ignored it to focus on the question.

I knew that he wanted to be my friend, but trust took time to build. We were on our way, but I knew it was going to take me longer than a trip to the zoo and a trivia night to trust him with the weight of my past.

***

"It was lovely to meet you, Addy!" Justine gushed, giving me a big hug and squeezing just a little too hard.

"Nice to meet you both, as well," I said warmly.

I was exhausted, but it had been fun to hang out with them. And with Bell.

I'd been surprised by how easily we got along. There was never any pressure when I was with him. Conversation was easy. He was charming, intelligent and respectful.

I'd found myself watching his face when he laughed, and his nose crinkled in a way that put a dimple above his eyebrow. He was captivating, and while my logical brain wanted me to run, something else was telling me that maybe he was worth letting into my life.

I turned to give Greg a hug goodbye and he instead wrapped an arm around my shoulder and started moving towards the cab that was waiting to take me home.

"I'm going to walk Miss Addy to her vehicle," he called over his shoulder. "Bell, be a dear and escort my fiancée to ours?"

I glanced back to see Bell's shocked face before Greg was hurrying us across the parking lot.

"Sorry about that," he said softly, releasing my shoulder. "I wanted to talk with you for a bit, but I knew Bell would never let me, so I had to steal you away."

Instantly my hackles raised, and my guard was up. Greg and Bell were clearly very close, and whatever reason Greg had for wanting to talk to me alone couldn't be good.

"Well, maybe it's better to respect what Bell would want," I said warily.

"Nah, he doesn't know what he wants," Greg waved a hand dismissively.

"But you do?"

Greg's eyes, which had been dancing with glee all night, turned serious.

"I know that Bell can't stop talkin' about you," he said softly. "And that he's never even tried to be friends with a lady before, so you must be somethin' pretty darn special."

I blinked. My throat went dry and my hands started to sweat.

"I'm not sayin' any of this to freak you out, Addy," Greg smiled. "I'm just sayin'…Bell's a good guy. One of the best, in my totally unbiased opinion. And I think you could be really good for him. He'd never say it, but he's so afraid of scarin' you off. He's got his own issues trusting women, but he seems to want to try with you. So, I guess I just wanted to tell you that you can trust him too, if you want to."

I was stunned into silence. How had this man been able to read me so easily? The entire night I'd thought he'd been laughing and throwing jokes around, not paying attention to me in any sort of serious way. But apparently, he'd been ingesting my entire life story without my knowledge or permission.

Suddenly, him and Justine being together made a lot more sense to me. And I could appreciate an overprotective best friend. I had one of my own.

While I was still trying to catch up, Greg studied my face for a moment and then patted my arm.

"Great meetin' you, Addy. See you soon!"

He took off at a jog across the parking lot to his car.

I climbed into the back of the cab, still trying to make sense of what he'd said. I gave the driver my address as my phone rang and I answered without thinking.

"Addy?" Bell's voice was small on the other end. "Addy, you there?"

"Hi, yeah, sorry," I said distantly.

"Did Greg totally freak you out?" Bell blew out a breath. "I knew he would do something stupid like this. Addy, I'm sorry for whatever he said. He doesn't know what he's talking about —"

"Bell," I interrupted before I could overthink anything. "Would you like to go for a run with me tomorrow?"

Bell was quiet on the other end. I knew he was processing the fact that this was *me* asking *him* to hang out with me, instead of the other way around, which is how it had been so far.

And I honestly couldn't say why I'd asked him, just that Greg telling me I could trust him really struck a chord. And I was tired of denying that I wanted to spend time with Bell.

Spending time with him and trusting him were two different things, but maybe one could lead to the other? Maybe it was like Laura had said? I couldn't fix my relationship issues on my own, and even a platonic relationship with a man would help. I enjoyed spending time with Bell. I liked being around him, and he made me feel safe.

"Bell?"

"I'd love to go for a run with you, Addy." He was breathless, but I could hear the excitement in his voice.

"Great," I said softly. "I'll meet you at the park tomorrow then. Seven A.M. sharp."

"See you then."

The line clicked off and the silence of the cab pressed down on me. I knew I'd just made a decision that would change me, and I was trying so hard not to be absolutely terrified.

Chapter Five

Bell

I didn't normally go running this early in the morning, but I wasn't about to pass up an opportunity for uninterrupted alone time with Addy. Especially when it had been her suggestion.

So, here I was, doing jumping jacks at the trailhead to try and work some energy into my body, when I saw her.

She had on baggy jogging shorts and an oversized T-shirt, her wild brown hair up in a bouncing ponytail. There was nothing revealing about her clothes, nothing suggestive in the way she jogged over to me with a small smile on her face. But she was the most gorgeous woman I'd ever seen. The world stopped when our eyes locked.

My heart started pounding in my ears, and I inhaled sharply. The cold morning air brought me back to reality and helped curb some of the panic that had just flooded my system.

As Addy got to me she was looking at me curiously, cautiously.

"Morning, friend," I said with too much enthusiasm.

She blinked at me before offering me a warm grin. "Good morning."

"I don't usually run this early during the week," I said as I gestured for us to start.

Addy easily kept pace with me. "I have to be at work at nine, so this gives me enough time to do the loop and make it back to my apartment in time to shower. I don't drive, so it's all about the bus timings."

I bit my lip to keep from smiling too wide. She was offering personal information. Not anything crazy, but more than she ever had before. The obvious follow up would be to ask why she didn't drive, but I knew her well enough by now to know how quickly she could clam up.

"At least the bus schedules around here are pretty consistent," I said instead.

She flashed a smile at me and then looked back at the trail in front of us.

"So, what's your time?" I asked.

"I usually average between a seven and eight minute mile," she said easily. I noticed she wasn't out of breath, and she had a steady stride. She could keep this pace for hours, I was sure. "You?"

Her question caught me off guard because I'd been watching her form, and when my eyes flicked up to meet hers, they were sparkling with mischief.

She thought I'd been checking her out, and she didn't seem to be offended by that. I filed that away for later and re-focused on the path in front of me.

"I'm probably about the same," I shrugged.

I was lying. I was a big guy who enjoyed more of a leisurely jog than an actual run, but I wasn't about to tell Addy that.

Her eyebrows raised as she appraised me.

"What?" Defensiveness creeped into my tone.

"Oh, nothing just..." she hesitated a moment, "you really run an eight-minute mile?"

"You don't believe me?" I laughed. How could she have seen through me so easily?

She laughed with me. "It's not that it's just... I mean, you're a big guy!"

"Oh, I know," I winked at her and was surprised when a giggle escaped her mouth.

The sound was like fairy bells to me. Magical. Rare. Something to be treasured.

She seemed to realize how out of character that was for her at the same time I did, and her mouth clamped shut and her gaze dropped to her feet for a moment.

There was that wall again. I'd seen it last night too. Every time she started to get comfortable with me the wall would go up and we'd be back to polite distance. Acquaintances, not friends. Not anything, really. Just two strangers who couldn't seem to stay away from each other.

I didn't know what the issue was, and I knew she wouldn't tell me unless she trusted me. I just wasn't sure how to make that happen.

My Pops always told me that there can be no trust without honesty. Maybe that's where I'd start.

"I don't usually time my runs," I admitted. "I like to jog when I need to work through things in my head without getting interrupted. It helps me get some clarity. So, I don't run as consistently as I'd like, but I do enjoy it."

Her eyes met mine again and there was a cautious sparkle in them. Feeling daring, I added one more thing.

"Also, you have a beautiful laugh."

Her eyes went wide and I watched her pupils dilate and pink spots appear high on her cheeks. God, she was gorgeous.

The panic that had welled up earlier hit me in full force now.

My throat felt tight and my chest pounded. I couldn't breathe as I watched her.

There was too much unsaid between us, but now was not the time to bring it up. Not when she was just warming up to me and I was in the middle of a mild panic attack because I had real feelings for a woman for the first time in my goddamn life.

She seemed to sense the change and gazed ahead, giving me a needed relief from getting lost in her eyes. Like some lovesick fool.

"So, if you don't track your times then you don't really know what your pace is, right?"

I managed to nod. Words wouldn't form around the lump in my throat.

"So, how about a race?" she suggested. Her tone was light, playful, but still careful.

I didn't know how she'd come to be able to read me so well, to know when I needed to move past something, but I was grateful for it in that moment.

We honestly hadn't spent that much time together, so could she just read me that easily? Or was I not imagining this connection between us? I needed to process this woman, and I couldn't very well do it with her bouncing along right next to me, so instead I forced a smile onto my face and nodded.

She grinned up at me and then pointed to a bench a little ways ahead.

"We'll start there, and the first person to finish the loop back at this bench wins, okay?"

I took a deep breath and nodded.

We hit the bench and Addy took off. She'd clearly been holding back, now outpacing me with ease. I watched her in wonder, the panic still there but mingled with intense longing.

I wanted her. I wanted to be her everything. I wanted to be there when she woke up and when she was sad and when she was happy and when she was silly. I wanted to figure her out. I wanted to know how she'd managed to climb under my skin and turn me upside down and inside out without lifting a finger. I wanted everything she was willing to give me.

Right now, that was friendship.

I could do that. I might have to lie to myself to make it happen, but I needed to keep her in my life.

I had never needed a woman in my life before. They didn't usually stick around, so I spent time with like-minded women. Women who wanted the same thing I wanted. No strings.

But as Addy ran away from me, I could see the strings binding me to her. Like I was her puppet.

Fear gripped my heart as the full weight of her presence in my life hit me.

I couldn't leave her alone. I couldn't be her boyfriend.

So. Friends it was then.

With an audible groan I dug my feet into the gravel path and took off after her. I had a feeling I'd be chasing her for as long as she'd let me.

***

Addy whooped and jumped as she passed the finish line a good hundred feet ahead of me.

I didn't care. Seeing her guard down, her cheeks flushed, her eyes sparkling. I wanted to capture it and never let it go.

I took a deep breath and reminded myself to cool it. I had to give her time and follow her lead. She deserved that from me.

"A well fought victory, ma'am," I put on a little more twang just to hear her laugh.

"You almost had me around mile four, I will admit," she

laughed breathlessly.

"Oh, come on now, you're being generous," I winked. "You slowed down to make me feel better."

She held up her hands. "I plead the fifth."

"That's what I thought," I sank down onto the bench and put my head between my knees, trying to catch my breath.

Suddenly, I felt her hand on my shoulder. I looked up and she was offering me her water with a small smile on her face.

I took it from her, very aware of the fact that she hadn't removed her hand from my shoulder, as we simply looked at each other.

Her body swayed toward mine, and I wanted to reach out to steady her. As my hand came up she took a hesitant step backwards.

I cleared my throat and took a sip of water. Then I stood and handed it back to her.

"I know you usually catch the bus, but could I drive you home?"

There it was again. That wall. Her face shuttered, and she looked a little lost. Sad.

"You know, I'm sorry, I totally spaced that I have to go meet my Pops for breakfast. I hate to take back the offer, but if I don't head straight there I'll be late, and that'll be my ass handed to me," I back peddled.

I gave her a quick smile before turning to finish the trail and head to my car.

"Bell."

I turned back and saw her fiddling with the chain of her necklace.

"Greg told me that I could trust you," she said softly. "At least, try to."

My throat went dry.

"I want to try, but I wasn't kidding about my issues.

They're...heavy," she sighed. "No one comes to my apartment except my best friend and my parents."

She walked toward me and rested a delicate hand on my arm for a moment before crossing hers over her chest defensively.

"Just so you know, it's not you." She twisted her mouth in an awkward attempt at a smile, and my heart broke for her just a little.

I lifted a hand slowly and traced her cheek with my thumb. "It's not you either, Adelaide," I said quietly.

"Bell –"

"Whatever happened to put you on guard like this," I said carefully, twisting one of her curls between my fingers, "is not your fault. And you're dealing with the consequences of it amazingly."

Her hand came up and stopped mine, her fingers curling around mine warily. Her eyes were shining up at me and I fought like hell to control myself so I didn't fuck this up.

"As your friend," I smiled at her and she had the decency to blush, "I've got your back. You're in control here, Addy. I could easily see us being more than friends, but I want to be in your life more than anything else in the world, so if friends is how you'll have me then I'm good. We're good."

She was silent for a moment, her fingers gripping mine. Then she squeezed and let go, stepping back a bit.

"I think we could be really good friends," she finally said.

I felt a brick land in my chest, but I managed to smile. I swept my arm in front of me.

"Friends at least let friends walk them to the bus stop."

She smiled sadly and then stepped next to me.

The fierce urge to hold her until all her pieces were back together overwhelmed me, but I settled for bumping her playfully with my shoulder.

As I watched her get onto the bus, I knew how hard this was going to be. But I also knew I didn't want to turn back.

60

Chapter Six

Addy

I spent hours during my days thinking about Bell. His warm eyes watching me when I talked, as if I were the most interesting person on the planet. The way his lips curled when he was smiling but didn't want to be. The way his eyes traveled down my body and sent shivers straight to my core.

The last couple weeks hanging out with Bell had been nice. After our run, we'd met up for breakfast, we'd gone to the Hartworth Farmer's Market, and we'd seen a free music in the park thing with Greg and Justine. As much as I told myself these weren't dates, everything in me wanted them to be.

It was challenging, fighting my body's ache for him. Trying to let my logical brain win instead of my fickle heart, who had proven its incompetence in the past.

I knew that I couldn't trust my heart. But even the clear-thinking side of me was finding it harder and harder to keep my distance from Bell.

I remembered the feeling of his hand on my cheek in the park, telling me I wasn't broken. Those hadn't been his actual words, but it was what had bounced around in my head the rest of the day.

So many people over the years had tried to tell me that it wasn't my fault. That I wasn't to blame. It had taken time, but I'd eventually believed them.

Even then, I'd always held onto the belief that, while it wasn't my fault, my experience with Derek had broken me. Turned me into someone unfixable. Life had seemed to prove that over and over. It had been years since I'd had a normal interaction with a man. One that didn't end in a panic attack, yelling, or physical violence. Hell, I had to practice being in public spaces alone.

The entire first year after the attack, I'd forced Raelynn to go with me everywhere I went. I'd taken her to all of my self-defense classes, until I knew who all of the people were and trusted them. I'd made her go grocery shopping with me, drive me to and from work. Through it all, she had never complained. She'd been there, a steady, comforting presence. But there was always a part of me that knew I was being a burden. That wished I could just be better.

Bell was breaking down the belief that still suffocated me that I was, in fact, broken. And I almost believed the way he seemed to look at me. Like I was something to be admired rather than pitied.

I thought about his eyes a lot. More than I cared to admit. The way they watched me, as if I were the most fascinating thing in the room. The way the sunlight caught them and melted the color into honey-tinged chocolate.

I was currently at work, staring blankly at my computer, thinking about those mesmerizing eyes.

I shook my head as I turned my attention back to the screen in front of me. The account I was working on wasn't complicated, but it did require my full attention, which it wasn't getting. That's why I was now an hour into overtime that I wouldn't be paid for.

I sighed and rubbed my eyes, grateful I hadn't worn makeup today so I could really sink my knuckles into them trying to banish the weariness that came from staring at a computer all day.

I glanced at my watch. Shit. I was almost late to meet Raelynn for dinner. Once a week we got together at an old diner downtown that we'd been going to since we were teenagers. I quickly packed up my things and hopped on the bus, getting to the diner a little after seven.

The nice thing about living in a place like Hartworth was that everything was pretty predictable. The busses were always on time, our booth in the diner was always open, and there were hardly any people out in the middle of the week.

As I was sliding into our booth, my phone dinged. My stomach sank as I pulled it out to see a text from Raelynn canceling on me. She'd also been caught up at work and wouldn't be able to make it out. I sighed. I could just go home.

Then, my stomach rumbled and I chuckled to myself. Fine then, I'd stay and eat. It's not like I had a ton of food at home anyway. I hadn't been grocery shopping in far too long. The diner was comfortable and familiar, and it would be good for me to eat a meal by myself.

As I lifted my head to flag down a server, a tall, hulking form caught my attention. Then my eyes met deep brown ones. Eyes that lit up when they landed on me.

Bell.

I smiled as he made his way over to me.

"What a coincidence, running into you here," he said, his deep voice dripping like velvet in my ears.

"Either that, or you're stalking me?" I said. I was mostly joking. Mostly.

"Chill out, darling," he chuckled, his drawl making my stomach flip. "I was supposed to meet Greg here, but he bailed."

"Funny, I was supposed to meet *my* friend here, and she also bailed," I arched an eyebrow.

He looked at the empty seat across from me. "Sounds like the universe is trying to tell us something."

Our eyes locked and a spark flew between us. Suddenly, it was hard to breathe. I looked down at my lap.

"Well, you might as well sit down," I said through shaky lips. "Friends can have dinner together, I guess, seeing as that's what we both came here to do in the first place."

He slid into the booth with more grace than someone his size should have.

"So, what do you normally order?" he asked, perusing the menu.

"What makes you think I've been here before?"

"You're not looking at the menu," he shrugged. "Either you're a regular and know the menu forwards and backwards, or you're way too particular about your diner food and are going to ask to custom order something." He lifted his eyes to mine and winked at me. "I have a feeling it's the former."

"Raelynn and I have been coming here since our junior year of high school," I said, fiddling with my necklace.

"So, you're a local girl then?" he asked.

I nodded. "What? Are you surprised by that?"

He looked at me again, his gaze soft. "We haven't really talked about much personal stuff. It's the first time you've really offered up something about your childhood."

"Oh," I looked at my hands in my lap. I hadn't realized I was so protective of my past that in the course of hanging out with Bell, I hadn't told him *anything* about myself.

"Hey, here's a thought," Bell said, closing his menu. "Let's order, and then let's play twenty questions."

"Twenty questions? What are we, twelve?" I laughed.

"I will have you know that twenty questions is a very adult game to play," he said sternly, pointing a finger at me while his eyes danced.

I rolled my eyes and swatted his hand away as the waitress came up to the table.

She flashed a smile at me, but when her gaze dropped to Bell I watched her entire demeanor change. She straightened her shoulders and flicked her long blonde hair over her shoulder, smiling at Bell with all of her teeth. Something inside me bristled at her obviousness.

"What can I get you guys?" she said, a small twang in her voice.

Bell hadn't taken his eyes off of me, which seemed to tame the strange beast this girl had awakened in my chest. He gestured a hand toward me, and the waitress begrudgingly looked at me.

"A short stack with sausage and hash browns, please," I grumbled, my manners present even though all I wanted to do was shove her through a wall.

She scribbled on her pad and then swung her hair over her shoulder again as she turned to Bell.

"And for you?"

"Same."

One word, but a smile stole its way onto my face. He wasn't giving her the time of day, and for some reason it made me want to dance.

She huffed but wrote it down anyway and stormed away.

"You were jealous," Bell said, his voice dripping with satisfaction as he studied my face.

"What? What are you talking about?" I hedged.

"You looked like you wanted to send that waitress through the window for flirting with me." He gave me a devilish grin.

I blanched. The window and the wall weren't too far away from each other.

"Don't flatter yourself, Bell," I waved my hand.

"I don't have to, you do it so well," he grinned, sending another wink my way. I hated how quivery his winks made my legs.

"So, twenty questions?" I asked, trying to change the subject.

"Yeah," he laughed, letting me off the hook. "You know the basic rules. We each get to ask the other person twenty questions, and the person has to answer them, or, if they want to pass, they have to perform a dare selected by the questioner." He fiddled with the saltshaker.

"I always played for shots, but I guess dares work too," I said, a sneaky smile on my face.

Bell's face grew mockingly serious. "Adelaide, we are in a diner. This is a family establishment, missy."

"Oh, please do pardon me, sir," I put on my best Southern drawl and watched as his eyes blew wide and his Adam's apple bobbed as he swallowed. I mentally filed that away for further investigation.

I felt myself smiling and realized that I was actually pretty relaxed. The diner was busy, people were talking and the staff were buzzing around, but I wasn't on edge. Crowds normally had every muscle in my body tense, but as I sat here with Bell I realized that I felt safe with him. I knew that if something were to happen, he would protect me. He'd defend me, just like he'd done the night we met, and in the park.

I blinked as this realization settled in. It had been so long since I'd felt safe with *anyone*. Let alone a man.

But as I looked at him, there were no alarm bells, pun most definitely intended. He'd been nothing but honest with me from the moment we met, and he'd been proving that I could trust him every moment since.

He'd agreed to be friends, he'd kept his distance, not trying anything funny at any point. I didn't miss the way his eyes watched me, but he'd also admitted that he was attracted to me. He was upfront about wanting to be more than friends, but still respected the boundaries I'd set.

The more time I spent with him, the more time I wanted to spend with him. Alone. Not in crowds of people or with friends, but just us.

I wasn't sure what to do with this information, but I also realized that I'd been quiet for a little too long, and Bell was watching me curiously.

I cleared my throat. "First question to the gentleman," I said, waving my hand at him.

His eyebrows pulled together, but he chose not to question it. He tapped his long fingers against his chin, and I was mesmerized by the action. I wondered if he knew how attractive he was.

"What's the most illegal thing you've ever done?" he asked.

"Wow, just jumping right in there, huh?" I laughed.

I knew the answer immediately, but I wasn't sure I should tell him it was breaking someone's nose in a bar fight two years ago.

"Um, probably skinny dipping in Mr. Randolph's pond when I was sixteen."

His mouth dropped open, but he quickly recovered. "Why were you —"

I shook my finger at him. "No follow up questions, that's part of the rules."

His eyes narrowed at my finger, and for a moment I thought he was going to grab my hand. But he didn't. Instead, he held his hands up in surrender.

"Fine, your question."

"Are you aware of how attractive you are?"

The question popped out of my mouth without my permission. I actually slapped my hands over my mouth in shock, which caused him to laugh. That deep belly laugh that had warmed me from the beginning.

His eyes held mine as he ran a finger along his bottom lip. He watched my breathing hitch, and his eyes flashed with mirth.

I guess that answered that.

"Your question," I grumbled.

"You find me attractive?"

I sighed. "I – yes, obviously."

He looked ridiculously proud for someone who knew how attractive he was.

"How long have you known Greg?" I asked.

"We've known each other since college and are starting a business together. Tonight was supposed to be a planning meeting, but Justine has a stomach bug or something."

I nodded.

The waitress showed up with our food, practically throwing my plate in front of me, but setting Bell's down quite nicely. I rolled my eyes as she walked away.

"Are you jealous of how the waitress is flirting with me?" Bell asked, mischief in his eyes.

I turned my eye roll on him, but answered honestly, "Yes."

He chuckled but dropped it. We both took a moment to test a few bites of food.

"What's your favorite sport?" I asked him.

"Football," he said, as though it were obvious. "I played in high school and college."

"That makes sense," I nodded. He looked at me curiously, so I clarified, "You're huge."

"I definitely am that, darlin'," he winked. Again.

I shook my head, but my lips betrayed me by turning up at the corners.

"What's your biggest fear?"

Such a simple question, a routine getting to know you question. People usually answered with the dark, spiders, heights.

But in an instant the sound of glass shattering echoed in my head and my breath started to pick up as I tasted the adrenaline.

I took a few deep breaths to refocus on the present and then took a large bite of pancake.

"Pass."

Bell watched me for a long moment, and then nodded. "I dare you to compliment the waitress."

My eyes bugged out of my head, until I remembered the rules. I shot him a glare, and then flagged down our waitress. Her eyes narrowed as she came over to us.

"You have beautiful hair, I just wanted to let you know," I said, feigning a smile.

She blinked and then gave me a small and confused, "Thanks" before walking away.

"Your question," Bell said.

I nodded. I needed to keep my questions light so that he would get the hint and not try to pry. I was having a good time, and I didn't want something to happen that would ruin that.

"Favorite toy as a kid?"

"Malibu Barbie," he said.

"Wh - "

"No follow ups," he smirked. "Longest relationship?"

My jaw clenched. "Pass."

His eyes narrowed and he fired off another question before I could stop him.

"Worst injury?"

"Bell," my voice was a warning.

"Biggest regret in life?"

"Knock it off, Bell," I growled at him, anger flashing through me.

"Why won't you date me?"

"That's enough," I snapped, slamming my fork and knife down onto the table.

"You won't talk to me about anything personal, Addy," he protested, his eyes locked on me.

"Then why don't you take the hint and stop asking personal shit?"

"Because I want to get to know you, because I *like* you."

"Well, don't."

"Don't what? Don't like you, or don't ask anything that would make you open up so I can get to know you better?"

"Both." I was angrier than I'd remembered being in a long time.

"You can't just hide from everyone, Addy. Eventually, you're going to have to trust someone, and I really want that someone to be me." His voice was hurt, and so were his eyes.

I blew out an angry breath and gathered my purse and jacket.

"That's not something you get to decide, Bell," I snapped, standing from the booth and storming out.

I heard him calling after me, but I saw the bus approaching and ran for it. It didn't matter where it was going, I just needed to get away from him.

＊

I was waiting outside of Laura's office building when she arrived the next morning. She looked shocked to see me, but politely

70

asked her receptionist to block out a half an hour of her morning so that she could speak with me.

The next thing I knew, I was pacing a hole in her rug and ranting.

"How could he think it was even *remotely* appropriate to ask me those questions? Obviously, he's not an idiot. I'm sure he's pieced together that I'm fucked up for a reason, but he just kept pushing. Okay, so maybe I overreacted when I stormed out, but I told him to stop and he just kept going. Kept digging into what is clearly not his to dig into. Where are the boundaries?"

Laura was quiet as she let me get it all out.

"And we were having such a good time before that! I just don't understand why he felt like he needed to ruin it."

I huffed an angry breath out and flopped into the chair across from my ever-patient therapist, who smiled at me softly and waited a moment before asking, "So, what exactly are you needing from me?"

I blinked at her. "I just... you were the only one that I thought of to talk to about this."

"Why didn't you talk to Bell?" Her voice was measured and calm. "I understand having a reaction last night, but why not reach out to him today and tell him why you reacted?"

"Because I'm pissed at him," I grumbled.

Laura nodded slowly and then clapped her hands together. "Okay, then let me ask this: Why are you so upset that Bell pushed your limits like that?"

"Because –" the word came out quickly, but there wasn't anything prepared to come next. "Because. Because we've hung out before this and he never asked, so why would he suddenly want to know about my past? There have been times when things have come up and he's had the sense before to drop it. Or change the subject.

He clearly sees how it affects me, so why would he want to bring it up now?"

"Why shouldn't he want to know? You've been spending time together; he wants to deepen the relationship. Part of that is learning about each other," Laura's tone was kind, but there was an edge to it that I'd never heard her use before. "You've said yourself that you didn't know anything about Derek before you jumped in. You've told me that getting to know people is now a very important thing to you."

"Yes, getting to know *them*, not having them pry into *my* dirty laundry," I bit out.

Laura arched a single eyebrow and crossed her arms.

I heard my words and groaned, dropping my head into my hands.

"I hear it, I do." My voice was sad. "I just don't know how to open up. It's terrifying to think about him knowing my past."

"What scares you about it?"

Blood pounded in my ears as I tried to imagine telling Bell about Derek.

"He could not want to be my friend anymore," I finally whispered. "He could reject me because I'm too broken."

Laura sighed softly and came around her desk to take my hands in hers.

"He could reject you," she said, her voice kind but firm. "He's a human being in his own right, and he could decide that he's not in a place to hold the space for you right now. It's a possibility."

"Tough love, thanks," I mumbled.

"But, Addy, he could take it in stride and be able to help you." Her eyes searched my face, trying to show me the sincerity of her words. "You'll never know unless you take the risk and open up to him."

"What do I do if he leaves?" I hated the broken note in my voice, but I couldn't stop it.

Laura squeezed my hand. "Then you march right back in here and tell me how fucking wrong I was."

That startled a laugh out of me. I took a deep breath and released it. I was still pissed, still scared, and still reluctant...but Laura had definitely given me something to think about.

Chapter Seven

Bell

I'd fucked up. It's all I'd been able to think about since watching Addy run from me last night. And I couldn't even pinpoint when I'd decided to be such a colossal dickhead.

Things had been going so well, and Addy had been relaxed, comfortable. Smiling and open with me. I thought it would be the perfect time to press her a little. Try to figure out why she was so guarded.

And it blew up in my face.

I'd watched her run on to the bus, and my instincts told me that wasn't even the bus she needed. She just wanted to get away from me. Badly.

Frustrated, I'd grabbed some cash out of my wallet and threw it on the table, storming out after my... friend?

I knew it was obvious that I wanted to be more than friends. I'd told her at least once every time we were together. But I'd been trying to respect her boundaries, never pushing her. Until yesterday.

Running into her in the diner had felt like fate. Like the universe conspiring to get us to spend more time together. And she'd been so comfortable with me, joking, flirting.

I growled as the midmorning sun blinded me while I drove to the old warehouse that was quickly turning into a beautiful restaurant space.

When we'd first found it, the city had just finished remodeling and restoring it. It had needed a bit more interior work to make it habitable for a business, but we'd gotten a great deal on the rent because the city was eager to have a fresh, young business in the space. Right at the end of the main street in downtown, it got a ton of foot traffic, and I just knew we'd be the new hot spot in Hartworth once we opened.

Greg was organizing tables as I made my way inside and poured myself a shot of whiskey.

"Whoa, man, it's ten A.M.," he joked, but when he saw how quickly I downed it he turned serious. "Hey, what happened?"

"I fucked everything up with Addy," I moaned, pouring another shot.

As I knocked the second shot back, Greg came over and took the bottle from me. "You and I both know that whiskey isn't going to help you right now."

"You're right," I sighed.

"Tell me what happened, man," Greg sat at the barstool next to me and waited patiently for an explanation.

"When you stood me up last night, I was already at the diner, and Addy was there too. So we sat together, and I got this dumb idea to play twenty questions, to try to get to know her better. She's been really guarded with me, keeping me at arm's length and never really telling me anything real about herself. Just surface stuff, favorite Mexican food, stuff like that. And she was so comfortable with me that I thought I'd try to push her a little, to get some deeper information. Get her to realize she can trust me and be vulnerable with me."

"And it totally blew up in your face?" Greg said knowingly.

"Yeah. She ended up storming out, pissed out of her mind," I sighed.

Greg was silent for a moment, just watching me. Then, he took a deep breath and squared his shoulders. I steeled myself. This was his fighting pose, the stance he took when he knew he was going to say something that I needed to hear but probably would hate hearing.

"Go on, just give it to me," I said miserably.

"You can't force somebody to open up to you. You can't make someone trust you. You have to earn it, and by prying you just showed this girl that maybe she shouldn't trust you. And if she's got issues anyway, you might have just made it worse," he said.

I knew he was trying to be gentle, but I hated that what he said made sense.

"What made you think that, out of everybody in her life, you're the one she has to open up to?" he asked.

I squeezed my eyes closed as images of Addy laughing flew through my brain. "I guess it's not so much that I thought she *had* to open up to me, it's that I *want* to be the one she knows she can trust."

Greg looked at me, and I shook my head.

"I think she was in an abusive relationship in the past, and it screwed up her trust in men," I admitted, hating the bile that rose in my throat at the thought of another man touching her, let alone hurting her. "I just... I just want her to know she can trust me. That I won't hurt her. That I'd never do anything to hurt her."

"I hate to break it to you, bud, but you just did," Greg said solemnly.

"Shit," I sighed. "What do I do?"

Greg let out a deep breath and poured me one more shot. After I'd let the liquid amber burn my throat, he clapped me on the back.

"The only thing you can do is prove to her that you're someone worth trusting," he finally said. "If you really like this girl, and I know you do, then you'll let her set the pace. You just... be there. No pressure, no pushing, just present."

I swallowed around the lump in my throat.

I could do that.

***

The next week was busy. We were less than five days from our soft opening, where our friends and family and press and other invited guests would come to the restaurant.

Our first test, and we were determined to pass with flying colors. And to do that, everything needed to be perfect. We were training staff, finalizing menus, setting up décor, and taste testing our first batch of ales from the new brewery equipment.

I'd had almost no time to focus on anything but the restaurant, but I'd still made time to send Addy a text every day. Just an apology, a different one every day, each one feeling like I was baring a part of my soul for her. She hadn't responded to any of them yet, but I was holding out hope.

The day before our soft open, I sent her another text.

Bell: I just want to say again how out of line I was. I am so sorry for pushing you and not respecting your boundaries. That was stupid, and I promise I'll do everything I can to make it up to you.

p.s. – I'm throwing a party tomorrow night, and I'd love it if you'd come.

By the end of the night, with no response, I knew she wasn't coming. I tried to hide my disappointment by throwing myself into last minute adjustments to the table linens and lights. It was midnight by the time I forced myself to close up shop and go home, not wanting to be burnt out for tomorrow.

I plugged my phone into the charger next to my bed and was just drifting asleep when I heard it buzz on the nightstand.

Addy: I can't make it tomorrow, but maybe we could go to the park on Saturday?

I smiled to myself. I didn't know why she was awake, but she'd finally responded.

Bell: I'll be there with bells on :)

The smile didn't leave my face as I drifted into sleep.

***

The soft launch had gone flawlessly. Every light, every glass, every table setting was perfect. Our families and friends had been beyond impressed with our work, and every reporter and critic we'd invited had given us raving reviews.

They loved the atmosphere, the vibe. They even loved our story, Greg's and mine, of two best friends who stuck together through thick and thin and were determined to come out on top.

And suddenly, overnight, we were the new hot spot for upscale casual dining in Hartworth. It was surreal. I'd known we would be, but seeing it actually happen was a dream come true.

There was something uniquely validating about creating something completely from scratch and seeing it play out exactly as you'd imagined it. For so many years this brewery had been our dream. And reality was better than our imaginations. It was everything we had ever wanted. Everything *I* had ever wanted.

And for all of that, I'd still felt like something was missing. Because the one person I wanted to share it with I was trying not to pressure. The one person that would have made me laugh and smile all night was still not really responding to my texts. I had the feeling she was waiting until we were together in person before she jumped back into our friendship, and I completely understood that. It didn't stop me from missing her something fierce every day.

But it was finally Saturday, and I walked into the park with a basket of food and a small bell pinned to my T-shirt, my excitement growing by the second.

I scanned the grass and finally spotted a head of wild, dark curls that shimmered in the sunlight.

I stopped a few feet from Addy, who turned as soon as she felt me approach. Her eyes were cautious, but there was a smile playing with the corners of her mouth.

We simply stared at each other for a long moment. There was so much unsaid between us, so much tension and heat. Her eyes flicked down my body, setting my nerves on fire. I watched as she swallowed and her eyelids fluttered. Her breathing picked up as our eyes met again, and every instinct in me was telling me to tangle my fingers in her hair and kiss her until we couldn't breathe.

I wanted to taste her again, to feel her body melt against mine like it had that first night we'd met. As we watched each other my mind was flooded with the urge to find out what sounds she would make when I slid my fingers along her stomach while kissing her neck.

I finally came back to reality, realizing that I'd been staring at her for far too long. I didn't know what to say to break the ice, so I said the only thing that had been on my mind from the minute she'd left the diner.

"I'm so sorry."

She blinked those blue eyes at me and my heart pounded in my chest.

"I know you are," she sighed. "And I forgive you."

"You do?"

"I wouldn't be here if I didn't," she teased.

All of the tension melted from between us, and I felt like I could breathe again.

Then she stepped aside to show a blanket spread on the ground with a bottle of wine and two glasses set out. "Looks like great minds think alike."

"It actually looks like we complement each other." I lifted the basket. "I've got food but no wine, and it looks like you brought wine and no food."

"Looks like we're a perfect match, then," she said softly. There was so much behind her words, and she avoided it by keeping her eyes glued to the blanket.

I watched her for a moment before setting the basket down and turning to face her.

"I know I've said it a lot over the last week, but I really am truly sorry, Adelaide," I said quietly. "I want you to know that I heard you. There are things you aren't comfortable talking about, and I will never push you on them again. Tell me when you're ready, and I promise I'll be there to listen."

She was quiet for a long moment before she took a step closer to me, reaching out to gently squeeze my hand.

"I'm sorry I kept you waiting a week," she finally said, her voice gentle. "I was really pissed."

"You had every right to be," I insisted. "I was an idiot."

"You were," she smirked. "But you also weren't wrong. I don't let people in. It's hard for me to trust people."

"I get that, I have my own issues. Hell, everyone has trust issues in some way or another," I parroted Greg.

A dry smile flickered across her face. "Can we just agree that, at least for now, we'll keep things surface level? Nothing too deep?"

"I promise, Addy, I won't push you anymore," I told her reverently. "I do want you to know that you can trust me, but I understand it'll take time. And I'll do my very best to show you every day that you can believe in me."

She searched my face, and then dropped her eyes to where our hands were still intertwined. She looked back up at me and her eye caught the bell I'd safety pinned to my shirt. A warm smile flashed across her face as she reached out to touch it with her delicate fingers.

"With bells on," she whispered.

"There's nowhere I'd rather be right now, Addy."

She looked up at me and I hadn't realized how close we'd gotten, because her body was brushing against mine.

I was too hot, flushed suddenly. I knew she felt it too because she took a quick step backward and bit her lip.

I watched her fiddle with her necklace, which I knew she did when she was nervous, so I cleared my throat and changed the subject.

"So, what do you do for fun?"

I sat down and poured us some wine, happy when she followed suit, sitting a few feet from me on the blanket. I tried not to squirm when our fingers touched as I handed her a glass.

She looked at me and her lips quirked into a smile. "MMA."

My jaw actually dropped. "You fight?"

"Pretty well, actually," she said, a faint hint of pride in her voice.

"Think you could show me some moves?" I was joking, but then her eyes lit up.

"For real?"

"I mean, yeah, why not? I'm a big guy, but I've never been much of a fighter. Might be useful to learn some tricks," I winked and took a sip of wine.

It was good. She had good taste. I hoped it was a good sign that she was choosing to spend her time with me.

She laughed and shook her head, her curls bouncing against her cheeks. "Well, maybe someday I'll show you."

I lifted my glass to her. "I'll hold you to that."

The sound of her laughter made my blood buzz in my body, and I realized that I needed this girl in my life. Even if she was just meant to be a friend, I didn't want to let her go ever again.

Chapter Eight

Addy

"Johnny has no idea what he wants when it comes to this wedding," Raelynn moaned as we flicked through photos of flower arrangements.

"Neither do you," I laughed, placing a sticker on a page with one I thought would look nice for the centerpieces.

"Exactly! That's the problem," she huffed.

I laughed and sipped my wine. "You know though, if either of you actually had any idea what you wanted it wouldn't have taken you so long to get together."

"You're right," Raelynn laughed. "I guess I'd just hoped that the indecision would stop there and that once we were at this stage we'd be on the same page."

I shook my head at her. "You love that you guys aren't on the same page. You disagree about almost everything, which is what keeps it exciting for you."

"The only thing we agree on is that we're madly in love with each other," Johnny's voice said from the doorway.

We looked up from our photobooks as he came in the room and lifted Raelynn from the sofa to pull her into a long, too hot to be doing in front of company, kiss.

I chewed on the inside of my cheek while refocusing on the flowers in front of me. When they finally broke apart, Johnny shot me a cheeky grin.

"Sorry about that, Ad, but I can't help myself," his Australian accent was always a little thicker when he was around Raelynn. I was convinced it was because he knew she thought it was hot.

"Oh, trust me, Johnny, I hear all about how you can't help yourself," I joked.

"So, my exploits are that good you just can't keep them to yourself, huh love?" Johnny teased Raelynn.

"Great, now I'll never hear the end of that," she sighed dramatically, a smile playing on her face.

Johnny and Raelynn settled on the couch and Rae sighed heavily again.

"Why don't we just elope?" Johnny said, half joking half hopeful.

Raelynn glared at him. "Because *someone* promised my mother that we'd have an actual wedding."

"One of my gravest mistakes," Johnny moaned.

I grinned, loving their banter. As much as I could see Raelynn eloping, I was selfishly happy they weren't. It meant I got to help my best friend plan her wedding, which I was enjoying even if she wasn't.

I flipped the page in the book of flowers I was perusing and stopped, my eyes widening.

"Hey, what do you guys think of these?"

I turned the book around and they both cocked their heads and studied the intricate gardenia bouquets for a moment.

"I like them."

"They're beautiful!"

They looked at each other in shock.

"Lady and gentleman, I think we've found your wedding flowers!" I said triumphantly.

Johnny whooped, standing to spin Raelynn around before bounding over to me and planting a wet kiss on my cheek.

I loved being around Raelynn and Johnny. They were two completely different people, but both were fiery and exuberant about life and that's what made them such a good match. They'd both been so against settling down with just one person, though, that it had taken them far too long to accept their feelings for each other. But together they just… worked. They made me believe that true love existed.

It had taken awhile for me to fully trust Johnny. He'd been with Derek's group the night that we'd met. He hadn't known him, so there was no blame to lay at his feet. He just made me remember things that I didn't want to sometimes.

But he'd proven to not only be madly in love with my best friend, but a loyal and true friend to me as well.

"Now we get to move on to the guest list," Raelynn said jovially.

She pulled out yet another binder and looked at me slyly.

"So, Adelaide," she hedged.

I took a deep breath and glared at her. I knew that tone.

"Yes, Raelynn?"

"Will you be bringing a date to our wedding, or do I have to put you at the singles table?"

"You wouldn't dare," I huffed.

"I might, if you don't have someone you'd want to bring."

I opened my mouth to tell her to fuck off, but before I could Bell's face popped into my head. My mouth clicked shut.

I wanted to bring Bell to my best friend's wedding? That was something very serious to me, and I felt like I'd been hit with a fast pitch out of nowhere.

Things with Bell were good. We'd made up from the diner incident and we were talking most days of the week, whether that be texting, calling, or hanging out. He was being a very good friend, respecting my limits and keeping things light between us. He was hell-bent on actually *showing* me that I could trust him. And I wanted to. I could feel myself relaxing more with him.

Maybe that's why I thought of him for the wedding. Because I knew it would be a stressful day, and Bell always made me feel safe.

"You're thinking about Be-eellll," Raelynn teased in a sing-song voice.

I blinked at her.

"What? No, I'm not," I snapped defensively.

"Who's Bell?" Johnny asked, plopping back down onto the couch and draping his arm around Raelynn's shoulders.

"Bell is this gorgeous man that's been courting our Adelaide here."

"He is not courting me," I scoffed.

"What else would you call taking you on very not-date dates and letting you call the shots? Giving you tons of space and time to get used to him, but keeping his intentions perfectly clear? Is that not what the Southern Belles would call courtin'?"

"Well, he sounds like a charmer," Johnny chuckled, but his eyes were watching me carefully.

Johnny didn't know all the details of what had happened with Derek, but he knew enough. And, in spite of how optimistic and easy-going he was about life, he was very protective of me.

"He's becoming a very good friend," I said pointedly.

"You can bring a friend as a date to a wedding," Raelynn chirped. "I'll just put you and Bell at our table for now, and if anything changes let me know."

"Changes?" I sputtered. "I haven't even decided to ask him to come. The change would be him attending in the first place, Lynnie!"

"Woah, woah, woah," Johnny said dramatically. "If this man is going to be coming to my wedding and sitting at my table with the Maid of Honor then I have to meet him first."

"No way," I said, just as Raelynn said, "Of course you have to meet him!"

"Guys," I began to protest when Raelynn cut me off.

"You've met his best friend, why can't Bell meet us?"

I didn't have a good answer to that. Bell had let me into his life, he'd told me things about himself, he'd introduced me to his friends. He was taking actions to show me that he wanted to be in my life in whatever capacity I was comfortable with. I, on the other hand, was clinging so tightly to my fears and doubts that I'd made it almost impossible for him to know anything about me.

But there were two things that I knew for certain about Bell: he made me feel safe, and I wanted to keep him in my life. I couldn't keep him if I didn't start trusting him.

And that meant letting him in.

"You're right," I finally said softly.

The atmosphere of the room changed quickly. Raelynn and Johnny were giving me their undivided, most serious attention. It was very rare that I conceded anything to them.

"Bell has become important to me, and I want him to meet you both."

I saw the couple across from me share a glance before they turned back to me.

"Game night?" Johnny suggested. His eyes were soft, and he reminded me why I was so happy that Raelynn had found him. He was a good person and he loved deeply, friends included.

"I think that would be great," I said after a deep breath. Now I just had to suck it up and invite Bell.

Chapter Nine

Bell

The brewery was a huge success.

After only being open a few weeks, we were booked solid for the next six months. We were in talks to start doing events; weddings, small concerts, trivia nights. Anything that we could we were trying to host.

This translated to a lot of work, but Greg was an incredible business partner. We split the duties of ownership so that we still had time to live our lives outside of work. He and Justine were diving into wedding planning, and I was loving getting to spend time with Addy.

I thought about her all the time. Throughout my day, whenever something reminded me of her, I wrote it down in a notebook. If we were dating, I would have texted her to let her know what made me think of her. But we weren't dating. We were friends. And I was trying so hard to respect that. But, if I was being honest with myself, I enjoyed having her in my life so much that I was happy to have any contact.

I was in the back office working on receipts when I saw her name light up my phone.

"Hello, there," I greeted her.

"Hey," she sounded a little breathless, and warmth slowly spread through my chest.

"What's going on?"

She hesitated. I could imagine her playing with the chain of her necklace.

"How would you feel about going to a game night my friends are hosting?" She sounded so hesitant, but I also didn't miss how hard this question must have been for her to ask.

This was big. This was her inviting me into her life. Wanting me to meet her friends. She was offering me a deeper glimpse into who she was, and there was no way in hell I was going to pass on this.

"I'd love to," I kept my voice light. "You should know, I'm pretty competitive."

"You'll get along great with Johnny then," she laughed. She sounded relieved, and I couldn't help but imagine the smile on her face. "It's Friday night, around six. Does that work?"

"I'll be there," I grinned.

"With bells on?"

"Always."

***

In yet another show of trust, Addy asked me to pick her up from work and take her to the game night. Neither of us said aloud that the implication was that I would take her home at the end of the night, which I knew was a big deal for her.

I couldn't quench the excitement that was growing inside my heart at these little signs that she was opening up.

I knew I wasn't completely delusional. The way I caught her

looking at me sometimes could melt the polar ice caps.

And she knew how I felt about her. I wasn't sure how much more sustained eye-contact I could handle before I lost my mind. So, these little shows of her confidence in me were making me downright giddy.

"You're awful fiddly," Greg joked as it neared the end of the day. "And you look downright handsome." His tone became suspicious. "What's goin' on with you?"

I blew out a breath and felt a smile steal onto my face. "Addy invited me to meet her friends tonight."

Greg's eyes grew wide and then he was grinning. "Congrats man! I told you, just be there and everything will fall into place."

"Yeah, yeah," I waved him off.

I grabbed my jacket from the rack by the door, and the last thing I heard before it clicked shut was Greg shouting, "I get to make a toast at the wedding, right?"

As I was driving to Addy's office, my stomach was in knots. I wasn't sure why I was nervous.

We'd spent time together before. But now that Addy was trusting me so openly the rules had shifted. I needed to continue to let her call the shots, to lead the way. Though, I had to admit I was excited about the direction she was going.

As I pulled up outside, she was coming out. I quickly parked the car so I could open her door for her.

My breath caught when she stepped into the setting sun. Her jeans were hugging her hips, drawing my eyes up her body to her beautiful smile and dancing eyes.

I managed to pull myself together enough to jog across the street to meet her.

"You okay?" she asked as I approached.

"Yeah, why?" I cleared my throat.

"Oh, you just had this look on your face," she said quietly.

Before I could answer, her eyes dropped to the pocket of my shirt and a wide grin spread across her face.

She reached up and jingled the bell that I'd pinned there and she laughed.

"You're ridiculous, you know that?" she said, some of the tension easing out of the air between us.

I captured her hand in mine and kissed it softly.

"You make me ridiculous," I said. It was the truth. Never in a million years would I have thought I'd be keeping bells on safety pins stashed in my car just in case I needed to get a girl to laugh. But here I was, bell on my shirt, and the most beautiful woman in the world laughing with me.

I led her to the car and helped her in. As I slid into the driver's seat, I had to stop and take a deep breath to steady myself.

"Are you sure you're okay?" Addy asked as she buckled herself in. "I've never seen you like this."

I turned to face her, my eyes boring into the side of her face. I knew I was being too intense, but her scent was filling my car and the thought of smelling her every time I got into the car for the next week was driving me insane.

"You're just so incredible that I forget how to breathe. I needed to take a second," I said honestly.

My voice was so soft I wasn't sure if she'd actually heard me. But then I heard her breath catch and it validated that I wasn't alone in this.

When she turned to look at me, her blue eyes cautious beneath her long lashes, something volcanic started bubbling inside me. She started to tremble, but there was no fear on her face. Her bottom lip disappeared beneath her teeth and I bit back a groan.

I turned quickly towards the windshield.

"We should go," I bit out. I shook my head and laughed at how flustered I was. "I don't want to make a bad impression on your friends."

She chuckled to herself and nodded. She gave me quiet directions and then we were off.

Addy broke the silence with a small sigh. "I should warn you about Raelynn and Johnny."

"That sounds ominous," I laughed.

"It's not *not* ominous," she smiled. "They're really good people, but they're very protective of me. They're also... a lot."

"Protective I respect," I assured her. "And I can handle a lot."

She grinned at me and visibly relaxed a bit into the seat.

"You should also know that they don't agree on anything, so they're constantly bickering. But that's just normal for them," she fiddled with her necklace, her head leaning back against the headrest. "They'd never let on, but they're really madly in love with each other."

"I think when two people are that in love there's nothing in the world that can hide it," I said warmly.

She was quiet for the rest of the drive, and got visibly more nervous the closer we got to the house. All I wanted to do was reach out and hold her hand, to reassure her that I was there for her, but I didn't think that was within the scope of our current boundaries.

When we finally pulled up to the house, Addy blew out a tense breath.

"I'm so sorry," she whispered, her voice shaking.

My brows pulled together as I turned to look at her. She was staring at her hands. I'd never seen her looking so vulnerable. Tears wavered in the corners of her eyes and it was as if by sheer force of will they weren't falling.

"What do you have to be sorry for?"

"I'm apologizing in advance," she huffed out a dry laugh. "I just know I'm going to be weird tonight. I don't... it's been a really long time since I've introduced anyone new to my friends, and I just want to manage your expectations. I'm going to be weird and I might shut down a little bit. I'm going to try not to, but I just... this is huge for me to have you here. And I *want* to have you here, I don't want you to doubt that at all."

She got quiet and then took three deep breaths before taking my hand in hers and looking up at me.

"I want to start letting you into more of my life," she confessed. "I like having you in my life, and I want to keep you here."

My heart hammered in my ears, and it took everything in me not to take her face in my hands and kiss her until she knew that she could keep me for however long she wanted.

I squeezed her hands in mine, trying to communicate everything I was feeling without saying anything. When she smiled at me, I knew she understood.

"Just don't make me play Monopoly, and I'm not going anywhere," I winked at her.

That got a laugh out of her. It was the first time I'd heard her really laugh, unrestrained and genuine, and I knew I'd remember it for the rest of my life.

"Come on," she sniffed. "Raelynn is probably at the window staring, so we might as well get this going."

I gave her hand one last squeeze, telling myself to keep control tonight.

***

"Uno!"

"Sorry, babe. Draw four."

94

"Bastard!"

"You weren't kidding, they're ruthless," I fake whispered to Addy as Raelynn and Johnny squabbled for the twelfth time that night.

Addy leaned into me, bumping her shoulder against mine as she laughed. The night had been fun so far. Raelynn was exactly what I'd expected from Addy's description of her. A little bombshell of a woman, she had no problem saying exactly what she was thinking at any given moment, and she honestly scared me a little. And her spitfire was complemented well by Johnny's own unique brand of slow-burning heat. Raelynn was like the first spark of a match and Johnny was the embers left over. They clearly loved each other, and it was nice to be around.

I glanced down at Addy. She had been more relaxed tonight than I'd ever seen her. After the initial introductions, she'd really started to enjoy herself. As I watched her, she sent a wink my way and then tossed down her last card, winning the game.

There was uproar and laughter from the other end of the table, and I found myself laughing loudly along with everyone else.

"You didn't want to warn me you were a shark before we picked this game?" I teased her.

"I've got to keep some mystery, don't I?" she joked back.

"I can't believe Addy didn't tell you that she's Game Night Master in this house," Johnny laughed.

"Is that so?"

"She's won every game night for the past three months," Raelynn nodded.

"Only because I keep my mind sharp and my glass full," Addy said as she stood with her empty wine glass in hand. "Refills, anyone?"

"I'll help," Johnny stood as well and ushered Addy into the

kitchen.

I didn't miss the significant look he shot Raelynn just before the door closed behind them.

I turned expectantly to the woman across from me. She was staring me down in a way that reminded me of a matador. I took a deep breath and braced myself.

"Addy tells me everything," she started. "I saw you guys the first night you met. It's clear that you care for her as more than just a friend."

"That's right," I confirmed. "I've always been up front with Addy about that, but I know she just wants to be friends and I'm honestly okay with that."

"How are you okay with that? No guy I've ever met would be okay with that."

I watched Raelynn carefully for a moment, considering my answer. It was clear that she was protective of her friend, and it made me happy that Addy had someone in her life that was so fierce. There were many things I could say, but as I studied Raelynn I knew that complete and total honesty was the only way to go.

"You've met Addy. You know how special she is. She makes every day brighter just by being in it, and after I found out what it felt like to be her friend there was no way I could let that go," I sighed. I ran a hand over the back of my neck. Complete honesty. "I've never been in a long-term relationship. I've never been friends with a girl like this before. There is nothing about this situation that I know how to handle. But I'm trying my damndest to show Adelaide that she can trust me. I don't know her past, but I do know her well enough now to know that's hard for her, and I'm trying to earn it. I'll never lie to her. I'll never hurt her. I can promise you that."

Raelynn watched me for a moment. Her face was so serious. My heart hammered in my ears, but I knew I'd been as honest as I could. Finally, a small smile spread across her face. It was tinged with sadness.

"Addy has a hard time seeing the good things in her life," she said somberly. "She doesn't believe she deserves to be loved. You and I both know how much she does." She took a deep breath. "I know that she trusts you more than she thinks she does. So, try not to let her get in her own way, okay? Be patient, but don't give up. Sometimes she needs to be pushed because she's too afraid to jump."

"Good advice," I dipped my head. "Thanks, boss."

"Damn right, I'm the boss," Raelynn laughed loudly.

The tension vanished and Johnny and Addy came back in with more drinks for everyone. Addy wasn't stupid, and I could tell she knew the talk we'd just had, but it seemed to put her more at ease.

The rest of the night went by in a flash of laughter, games, and stories. Before I knew it, I was pulling up to the curb outside of Addy's apartment building. I got out to open her door for her, and she rested her hand on my arm as I helped her out of the car.

I cleared my throat as I let her go, hating the feeling of her skin leaving mine.

"Well, Miss Adelaide, it was a lovely night," I put a little more drawl than normal into my voice just to watch her cheeks flush. "Here is where I leave you."

"Why, thank you Mr. Bell," she lilted, and my pants suddenly were a bit too tight. The smirk on her face told me she knew exactly what that little accent did to me.

"You've been a perfect gentleman."

"I'm always a gentleman," I pretended to be offended so that I could hear her laugh.

After her laughter softened, she looked at me.

Those eyes, so serious. I wanted to reach out and trace her cheek. I managed to keep my hands to myself. Barely.

"You're incredible, Bell," she said softly.

"You deserve nothing less."

She bit her lip, looking indecisive, before stepping close and pressing her lips to my cheek. It was over so quickly, but her scent lingered in the air around me and heat from her kiss spread down to my toes.

"Goodnight, Bell."

She backed towards the door slowly. Her eyes were watching me, waiting to see what I was going to do.

My brain was curious about that too. Every molecule in my body was screaming at me to follow her. To take her in my arms and kiss her until all the pieces of her heart were welded back together and we could live happily ever after.

Finally, after considerably too long and over the sound of my pulse in my ears, I managed to say goodnight before getting back into my car.

I watched to make sure she got inside her building before driving away.

Something was tightening inside of my chest as the car sped through the night, and I couldn't name it. It was hot and heady, but light and fresh all at the same time. It made me want to shout and be still. I'd never felt it before in my life, and I didn't know what to do with it. The air in the car was too thick to breathe, so I rolled the window down, but the night breeze did nothing to calm me down.

Was this what it was like to be falling in love with someone? It felt like the easiest thing in the world to tell myself I was falling in love with Addy. But the logical part of me knew that it made no sense. I didn't know the most important parts of her. But I knew her heart. And *that* was beautiful.

I had never believed in love. Romantic love. Sure I'd seen it. Greg and Justine were maddeningly in love. But I didn't think it was a part of my genetic makeup. Yet, there I was, flustered as all Hell over a simple kiss on the cheek.

Confusion raced around in my head. Joy, laced with mistrust and sprinkled with insecurity, pounded in my chest. In that moment it felt like I knew everything and nothing all at once.

The only thing that was clear to me was that I needed Addy in my life. For as long as she'd have me.

Chapter Ten

Addy

"Hey." Julia's voice pulled me out of the file that I was trying desperately to concentrate on.

"What's up, Jules?"

"We're still on for Friday, right?"

I blinked at her in confusion. "What's happening Friday?"

"Our double date!" She sounded a bit exasperated with me. "We set it up weeks ago, remember?"

As soon as she said it, I did. I also remembered how little I'd wanted to go then, and after spending time with Bell I wanted to go even less.

"Right," I hedged.

Julia saw my hesitation and crouched beside my chair. "No. Addy. You promised. You can't back out now, otherwise he won't go! He's crazy shy, but it's actually so adorable on him. Please, please, please!"

I sighed. "Can we just make it really clear to his friend that this isn't a date date? I don't want to go on a blind date where the guy thinks I'm going home with him at the end of it. But I'll go hang out so that you can have your date."

"Totally fair! I'll make sure that's really clear," she chirped.

"Okay, then yes we're on for Friday."

"Yay!" she clapped her hands together. "I will take care of everything, you just have to show up and eat free food, okay?"

"Promise?"

"I promise."

***

I sighed and stared at my reflection in the mirror. It was Friday night, and I was getting ready for this double "not-a-date" date.

I'd told Bell about it. I wasn't sure why I'd had so much anxiety over telling him, but I knew that I needed to.

After game night something had shifted with him. He'd meshed so well with Raelynn and Johnny. He fit into my life so easily. Not only fit in, but made it considerably better.

There had even been a moment, when we'd been saying goodnight, that I had almost confided in him. Told him all about my past. Confessed why I was so hesitant to date, why I had such a hard time trusting people.

I was even considering the possibility of maybe asking him for a date, if he still wanted to after hearing about my past. And there was no denying that, even after a few weeks, I was still as drawn to him as I had been that first night in the bar.

Every time he was around me, I had a hard time breathing and controlling my heart rate. There was just something about Bell... I felt like we'd been tethered together from the moment we first saw each other. When we were apart there was tension in my chest, like the tether was stretched too far for comfort. And when he was with me nothing else in the world seemed to bother me.

I'd realized that night that the only thing standing in the way of me and Bell being together was *me*. I knew that I was in total control of where our relationship went from here. And I knew where I wanted it to go, if I could just get out of my head and take the leap.

Which is why I'd known I needed to tell him about tonight. I told him that it was just a favor to a friend, nothing more. And he'd been so gracious about it. He hadn't even questioned why I'd felt the need to tell him, which told me that he could also feel the shift.

It was like climbing onto the railing of a ship, trying to decide whether to jump into the ocean or get back on the deck where it was safe. Something had to happen soon.

I shook my head and focused on the night ahead of me. I needed to be present for Julia. It would be a terrible double date if my head was off in the clouds with the man who was slowly breaking down all my walls.

I turned to examine myself in the mirror. The dress was too much. Julia had brought it for me today at work, telling me we were going to a swanky new restaurant downtown and that she didn't trust that I would have something to match the dress code.

She wouldn't have been wrong. I had maybe six outfits total, and they were mostly for work. When I was at home it was strictly sweatpants and tank tops. And a sweatshirt in the winter.

The dress she'd brought me was a deep blue that made my eyes look like a storm. It looped in a small collar around my neck, which attached to a plunging V. The flared skirt was flirty, offering glimpses above my knee, and made of delicate layers of chiffon.

I looked amazing in it, to be fair. But I knew it was probably expensive. I put on my only pair of heels, stilettos that hardly saw the outside of my closet. They made my legs look ten miles long, and the way the skirt showed off my thighs brought a small smile to my face.

My dark chestnut hair was naturally curly, fell to my shoulders, and had lovely volume if I put the right product in it. I scrunched the curls and crossed my fingers that they would look decent instead of frizzy.

I kept my makeup minimal, light eyeshadow and mascara, lip balm instead of lipstick. I didn't like the unpredictability of lipstick, especially when eating.

I turned once more in the mirror, appreciating the curve of my hips and the flow of the dress down my body.

Okay, maybe the dress isn't so bad, I thought to myself, twirling around.

It wasn't often I dressed myself up, but tonight I knew I looked amazing. My last thought before I left was that I strangely wanted Bell to see me looking so good.

***

The restaurant was indeed "swanky". It was really the only word to describe it. It was an upscale brewery, connected to a classy eatery with a long marble bar in the back. Everyone was dressed like they were going to a cocktail party instead of what was, essentially, a high-end pub.

In one half of the warehouse space was the brewery itself, with large tanks and walking tours and tastings of the newest ales they were producing. A wrought iron fence wrapped in ivy separated the brewery from the restaurant.

The dining room itself was magical. Fairy lights glittered in the high ceiling, and bare, warm lightbulbs hung from black cords over each table. There were ivy and potted plants along all of the walls, except the back where the long bar was. Each table was dressed in off white linens and mason jar candles.

The whole thing had a rustic, outdoorsy feel to it, yet no one, in their cocktail attire, was overdressed. A stage sat in the farthest corner of the room, near the bar, and a jazz band played softly. The ambience was mesmerizing, and it relaxed me as soon as we were ushered into the space by the hostess.

Julia was looking flawless, her long dark hair done in big curls that swept down her back. Her dress was cream, setting off her long, tanned legs and dark eyes. She was stunning, and I'd told her so about four times already.

She was also incredibly nervous. I thought it was cute, to see her so worked up over some guy. It had been a long time since a guy had made me nervous like that, since I'd wanted to look good for someone. I resolutely decided not to think about Bell in that moment.

She spotted our dates at a table against the wall. They stood as we approached, and I smiled politely.

"Addy, this is Aaron, my date. We met each other at a convention last year and have been pen pals ever since. And this is Michael. He's a friend of Aaron's from work," Julia gushed as she did the introductions.

"You ladies look lovely," Michael said, kissing the back of my hand softly.

My eyes narrowed at the touch. I'd hoped Julia had been clear about my intentions for the night, because the way Michael's lips lingered gave me doubts.

Aaron echoed the sentiment, but it was clear that he was painfully shy, as Jules had mentioned. He clearly had wanted Michael to come along to spur conversation, and Michael, it seemed, was more than up for the task.

Before we had even ordered appetizers, he had been talking non-stop about their work. I tried to follow along, but I found myself nodding out of courtesy rather than interest. Their job sounded boring as hell, and that was saying something seeing as Julia and I worked in finance, arguably one of the least intriguing industries.

After at least fifteen minutes of pretending to pay attention I finally just gave up. I found my gaze wandering around the restaurant. I observed couples laughing, and friends eating, all immersed in their own stories.

I watched as an older woman's face lit up when the band started a new song. It sounded like a big band song from the twenties, and her husband immediately grabbed her hand and pulled her out onto the little dance floor. They swayed in each other's arms, looking for the whole world like they were the only people left on Earth.

I found myself smiling, wondering when they'd met, how their lives together had been. I wondered how they were still so in love.

I watched them for too long, probably, and when the song came to an end, they shared a tender kiss. My heart ached in my chest with an emotion that I was too afraid to name.

"So, do you have any hobbies, Addy?" Michael's voice jolted me back to the table I was at. Back to reality.

I blinked as I processed the question.

"I do MMA." Was the only answer I could think of.

"Wow, MMA?" Aaron asked, tearing his gaze away from Julia. I could tell he was absolutely besotted with her.

"Yeah, just sort of something I fell into," I sipped my wine. I hated talking about myself with strangers.

Michael snorted in disgust, and I glared in his direction.

"Problem, Michael?"

He heaved a long-suffering sigh, and I knew I was about to hate whatever came out of his mouth.

"Women who fight MMA are basically dudes. There's nothing attractive about them at all. Why would any man want to date a woman that could beat them up? Women are supposed to be submissive, subservient, reliant on men for their care and protection.

It's not attractive, Addy."

My head slowly cocked to one side as I stared at him. Had he actually just said that? Did those words honestly just come out of his mouth?

Before I could stop myself, I was gathering my purse, draining my glass, and standing.

"Wait, Addy, where are you going?" Julia said in a panic.

"Jules, you and Aaron seem to be getting along just fine, and Michael and I seem to have diametrically opposed viewpoints on what a woman needs a man for," I said in a rush.

I really didn't want to be rude, but I couldn't sit here and pretend to listen to another word out of that pig's mouth.

"It seems to be his opinion that a woman should sit down, shut up, and suck his dick when it pleases him. It's my opinion that a woman in any position close to Michael's dick should bite it off."

His face blanched and his hand instinctively dropped to his lap. I bared my teeth in what I could only hope came across as a semblance of a smile.

"Have a good night, everyone."

I started to leave, and then realized that if I did that then this place would be tainted. It was too beautiful of a restaurant to have such a bad experience. I would *not* let some ineffectual luddite ruin the magic that was my new favorite spot downtown.

I made my way across the dining area to the bar. I was fuming, and I was silently hoping that the older couple would get up and dance again so that I could get lost in the fantasy of their romance.

I slammed myself on to a bar stool, trying to rearrange the chiffon to lay delicately across my lap. I was so riled up I wasn't sure if I succeeded.

The bartender's back was turned, and I huffed for a moment before calling to him, "Blue Label Whisky, on the rocks." I turned and saw Michael slinking out the door. "Make it a double."

"Sure thing," a honey smooth drawl answered back.

I turned slowly in my seat and saw Bell grinning at me from the other side of the bar.

"No way," I found myself grinning back.

"Way," he teased.

"You work here? What are the odds?"

"Well, I don't just work here, Addy," he said smoothly. He grabbed the whisky bottle from the top shelf and poured it in the glass without looking to see how much he was pouring. "I own the place."

"Seriously?" My mouth fell open as I looked around again. I shook my head, and a small smile crept onto my face. "I should've guessed. This place has Bell vibes written all over it."

"Why do you think it's called The Bell Tower?" he laughed and handed me my drink.

I rolled my eyes. I hadn't even put two and two together.

"Well, it's a gorgeous space, you've done really well with it," I complimented. I hoped he could hear how much I meant it. "How has this never come up?"

He gave a half shrug. "We've kept it surface level. Which has been fine, don't get me wrong. But this is something really important to me, so I didn't think it was on the table for discussion. Although, I did invite you to the opening."

A flare of guilt hit my stomach, and I fiddled with my necklace. Bell, who could read me so well, suddenly let out a warm laugh and changed the subject.

"Your first time here?"

"That obvious?"

"Repeat customers know to order the House Porter, it's what we're known for," he winked at me.

I laughed as I felt the stress of that horrible date melting away. It was so easy to be with Bell. He made me so comfortable.

"Well, it was a whisky night, sorry. Next time I'm here I'll know what to order," I winked back at him and took a sip of my drink. The burn felt good and sent warmth through my veins.

His eyes looked concerned. "Wasn't tonight your not-date double date?"

I sighed. "Yep. The guy her date brought along for me ended up being a misogynistic asswipe, so I called it a night. I was going to leave, but there's something about this place. I didn't want him to ruin it for me, so I decided to stay a bit."

"You really have terrible luck with men, don't you?"

I chuckled darkly, my mind flashing to ambulance lights and doctors. "You have no idea."

He looked at me for a moment before pouring himself a glass of whisky and setting it next to mine on the bar.

"Give me two seconds," he said, his voice soft.

I watched him walk over to the other bartender and they had a short conversation. Then he caught hold of a waitress and when they were through speaking, she traded her apron for a towel and came behind the bar to take over for him.

He made his way to me and sat down. He pulled my chair closer to his, but still with enough space that we weren't exactly touching. I could feel the heat of his body though, almost taste the pulse of his heart.

He lifted his glass and we drank silently for a moment.

"Can I ask something, as a friend?" He finally broke the silence.

My eyes narrowed suspiciously, memories of twenty questions putting my guard up. "I reserve the right not to answer but go ahead."

He chuckled softly and then looked hard at me. "Why don't you want to date anyone right now?"

I sighed. I knew he wouldn't just let it go. But there was also a part of me that was screaming to just tell him already. If anyone might not run away, it would be Bell.

"This feels like there's a hidden motive behind this question," I evaded out of habit.

"The motive's not hiding, Addy," he said, his tone a little harder. I could tell it was taking all of his self-control to stay light with me. "I've made where I stand perfectly clear. I want to date you. But I'm fine being friends because that's what you're comfortable with and I want to keep you in my life. But as your friend, and as the guy you don't want to date, I kind of want to know the reason why. We've been spending a lot of time together, and I just... I feel like it's something I might be able to help with, that's all. As a friend."

I took a deep breath and stared into the brown liquor in my glass. This was the moment. Did I jump off the railing and into the water? Or step back onto the safety of the deck?

Bell had been so patient. And even now he wasn't pushing for information. He was genuinely concerned and wanted to help me. How he thought he could help I wasn't sure, but I knew his motivations were pure. I also knew, deep down, that I wanted to tell him everything.

The problem was that I hated talking about this. In fact, there were only three people on the whole planet who knew anything about what had happened with Derek, and I hadn't even wanted to tell two of them.

"You don't have to tell me," Bell conceded. "I just... sometimes, when you think nobody's watching you, you look so sad. I hate seeing you like that."

"You don't even know me," I whispered, still unable to look at him. "And I know that's my fault, but still. You don't."

"But I want to. I want to know everything about you, Addy."
He blew out a deep breath and shifted towards me. The heat of him
invaded through the layers of cloth between us, and I found my body
mirroring his. "Honestly, I can't stop thinking about you. You're the
first thing I think of in the morning, and the last thing I think of
before I go to sleep. And I dream about you. Every night. And it's
more than a little insane, because we haven't known each other that
long. I sound crazy, and obsessive, and like a total nutjob, I know,
but that's the facts of it," he sighed.

I could feel his tension. I knew how much it had taken for him
to tell me that, to be vulnerable like that.

I closed my eyes. How could I tell him that I felt the same? That
everything he'd said I'd felt too? I didn't have the words for it like
he did. I wasn't eloquent, and I wasn't vulnerable. But for him I
desperately wanted to try.

I turned to look into his pained eyes. He was waiting for me to
say something. To shoot him down, probably. To run away, like I
had so many times before.

But, looking at his face, there was a soft voice in my soul telling
me it was time. To have him know everything. I wanted to be laid
bare for him, in more ways than one. I'd never wanted that before,
and it was fucking terrifying.

Every instinct in my body was telling me to run. To get as far
away from this man as possible. My mind was screaming at me –
don't let him hurt you! You can't let him in, he'll only hurt you! But
my heart...oh, my poor, foolish heart...wanted to give him
everything.

Raelynn's words from the night I met Bell rang in my ears.
*"You're allowed to be loved. You're not a burden, and your past is
not a non-starter. Not to the right person."*

110

Could Bell be that person?

He was still anxiously waiting for me to say something.

I looked back at my drink.

I'd decided. Time to jump.

I downed the liquor in one gulp. Then, I grabbed his and downed that too.

I looked at him and gently took his hand.

"Take me home, and we'll talk about it."

My voice was husky from the alcohol, and I saw his eyes flash. I finally figured out what that look was, the one I'd seen cross his face at least once every time we'd been together.

It was desire.

He wanted me just as badly as I wanted him. But he needed to know me first. That's what tonight would be about. Him knowing me. Then, he could decide whether to run or not.

I watched him swallow, and then he silently took my hand and led me from the restaurant.

Chapter Eleven

Addy

The drive to my apartment was silent, save my quiet directions. He opened my door for me, kept a respectful distance as we went to the front door.

I hesitated with the key.

A man had never been inside this space. My apartment was a reflection of my mind, of who I was at the core of my being. I'd always felt that someone could walk into my space and know me in an instant. I shook those thoughts off. Tonight was about being vulnerable with Bell. He'd been open with me, and I wanted to be open with him.

He was quiet as we walked through the doorway.

My apartment was spacious and open, the entryway leading right into the kitchen and living room. The single bedroom was down a short hall, with the attached bathroom. There were floor to ceiling bookshelves along one wall of the living room, large sliding glass doors leading to a balcony on the other, and a small TV in the corner, angled toward the couch. Knick knacks and photos covered most of the extra shelves.

My kitchen was tidy, almost immaculate. The one space in the apartment that I kept religiously clean.

My whole life was laid bare in this place. You could tell who the people of importance were in my life by how many times they showed up in frames. The books that I read most were all eye level and well-worn. There was a blanket draped across the couch and a few sweatshirts strewn about – I was constantly cold.

I looked around and realized that I had never noticed how much of myself I had actually put into this place. It felt…strange, allowing Bell to see me like this. Intimate almost. More intimate than I'd been with anyone in a long time. My heartbeat pounded in my ears as I fought back the panic that was rising in my chest.

He took it all in as I stood there, waiting for the judgment. But it never came. He looked around the room and then turned and focused his gaze on me.

I was feeling raw already, like an exposed nerve.

"Can I get you something to drink?"

"Whatever you're having is fine," he said with a soft smile.

I pulled out a bottle of my favorite wine and filled two glasses generously.

He laughed when I handed him his glass and led him to the couch. "You'd make a terrible bartender, Addy."

"Well, it's a good thing I'm not," I said, perhaps a bit more snappishly than I should have. I sighed and rubbed a hand down my face as I sank down onto the cushion.. "Sorry, I'm just…really nervous."

"Hey." He sat at the other end of the couch and reached over the space between us to rest his hand lightly on my knee. "I'm not going to judge you, Addy. Ever. I promise."

"I'd hold that promise until I'm done talking," I muttered. I looked down at his hand and slowly covered it with mine.

He was so much bigger than me, and normally that would

frighten me. But he was so gentle. Such a good soul. I trusted him. I didn't trust anybody, but I wanted to trust Bell with everything.

Without looking up from our hands, I started.

"I fell in love with my ex too fast. Like, way too fast. After a few dates, I was madly in love with him. We moved in together after a month. I had been so caught up in this…whirlwind romance that I hadn't noticed his…aggression. He had a short fuse, and a hot temper, and he flew off the handle about things. Small things. But I was so blinded by what I thought was this mutual, all-consuming love, that I didn't notice.

"When you live with someone though, it changes the dynamic. We were around each other all the time then, and he stopped trying. He stopped with the romance and the passion. He expected me to cook for him, clean everything, and to be at his beck and call sexually. When things weren't done to his standard, he got pissed."

I saw the muscles in Bell's jaw tighten as he saw where the story was heading. But he didn't tense his hand or move from his position a few feet from me.

I realized, as I came to the next part of the story, that I wanted him near me. I wanted him to know that I wasn't afraid of him. I wanted him to feel the trust I was placing in him. I scooted closer to him so that our knees touched and intertwined our fingers.

"A few months after I moved in, I'd gotten caught up at work, running behind on a project. I got home after him, and he'd been drinking."

Wasn't that how it always went? I sighed. I knew that Bell could probably guess the rest, but I wanted him to hear it. I wanted to tell him.

"He flipped out. I'd never seen him so angry. He was throwing shit and flipping tables. I was screaming at him to calm down, and I went and locked myself in the bedroom, but that only pissed him off

114

more."

I realized that my voice sounded clinical, but I couldn't stop to feel the emotions I'd felt in that moment. It would be too much; I had to keep a distance from it.

"He broke down the door and threw me into the dresser. The mirror shattered on top of me and cut my face. Then he grabbed my arm and twisted it behind my back. He broke it in two places, almost dislocated my shoulder. Then he threw me on the ground and kicked me until I stopped moving. I don't know if it was instinct, or what, but I knew that if I stayed still, stopped fighting back, he'd leave me alone. It worked. I was barely conscious, but I managed to get my phone out of my pocket and call nine – one – one."

I took a breath and peeked up at Bell. He was stoic, and I could tell he was trying very hard not to have a physical reaction.

I needed to be closer to him. I set my wine down on the coffee table, and he did the same. Then, without hesitation, I climbed into his lap. He wrapped his arms around me and settled them against my lower back, cradling me to him. I could feel how much he'd been wanting to do this, and I hadn't realized how much I'd needed this.

This closeness.

"I spent two weeks in the hospital recovering. I broke up with him then and there. My whole world fell apart. I realized that while I was in love with him, deeply, he was in love with the idea of me. I pressed charges, but he just disappeared. I haven't seen or heard from him since.

"When I was medically cleared, I started taking self-defense classes, and I joined an MMA gym. And I started running. My therapist says I have PTSD, which I guess makes sense. I still see her twice a month. Her, my mom, and Raelynn are the only people who know the full story of what happened with Derek." I paused and looked into his deep, understanding eyes. "Well, now you too, I guess."

We sat in silence for a moment, just watching each other, before I took a deep breath and ducked my head into his chest, knowing I couldn't look at him for the next confession.

"I don't think I know what love is, Bell. I thought I did, but I know that what Derek and I had wasn't really love. And because I don't know what it is…I don't know how to give it, and I don't know how to receive it. I'm very guarded, and I get nightmares, and I hate having other people take care of me. I don't trust it. When people are nice to me, I just keep waiting for the other shoe to drop.

"I made a promise to myself, lying in that hospital bed, that I wouldn't be with someone again until I *knew* them. Until I knew everything about them, their traits, their hobbies, their habits. How they treat small animals, how they travel, how they greet retail workers. How they live, how they grieve. Until I know someone's soul is good, I don't know that I can trust them, and I don't know that I can love them. And I can't *be* with someone…physically, until I know that I'm in love with them, and that they're in love with me. Irrevocably."

I waited in silence as he processed this. I knew it was a lot to take on, and that it wasn't something that most sane people would be willing to take on. As the silence stretched, his grip on my body never wavered. The longer it went, the more I could feel the self-doubt starting to creep in.

I pushed myself away from him and looked down at my hands.

"I know it's a lot, and it's why I said I couldn't date you. Because I don't even know what that would look like…and I know that it's selfish of me, but I do like you. I haven't been able to stop thinking about you either…at all…and it's really scary. And I understand if you want to walk away. You can leave right now and never come back and I will not blame you for it. I'm a fucking broken mess, Bell, and I can't ask you to take that on."

Finally, a tear fell onto my folded hands as I realized what letting him go meant. And how badly I wanted him to stay.

My sniffles filled the silence as I fought to control my tears. Slowly, deliberately, so as not to scare me, Bell reached out his hand and lifted my chin so that I had to look at him.

His eyes were endless pools of compassion. He gently wiped my tears and took my face in both of his hands. Then he kissed my forehead and pulled me into his chest. He wrapped his arms tightly around me, and I could feel him vibrating.

It was like he was trying to heal my soul with his own. Trying to send some of the goodness that was him into me. He was warm, and sturdy, and he held me like I was precious. I felt his lips on my hair, and for some reason that's what did me in. It was so gentle, so loving, so soft.

I sobbed into his chest. For the first time since my first few weeks of therapy, I allowed myself to feel the fear, and the anger, and the disgust with myself. I felt my heart breaking all over again. But this time I wasn't alone. Bell's arms held me tighter as I fell apart. Like he was determined to hold me together, and if he couldn't then he would put the pieces back in place as best he could. But most importantly, I realized through the haze of my grief...he stayed. He was still there, still holding me, even as I ruined his shirt with my tears.

Eventually, the tears ran out, and I registered that he was speaking. I tried to focus on his words, but they were so soft that I had to force myself to take calming breaths so I could hear him better.

"It's okay. You're not broken. I'm not going anywhere. I'm here. You're not alone. I'm here. Addy, I'm here."

A litany. For me.

I didn't know how long we stayed like that, him whispering comforting words into my hair, me holding onto him like a lifeboat at sea. Finally, I felt myself drifting to sleep. My breathing slowed, and my mind, exhausted, went blank.

I felt him lifting me, carrying me to my bed, and tucking me in. He didn't undress me, he didn't linger. He placed a soft kiss on my forehead and swept my hair from my face, and then I heard him leave the room. In the far corner of my mind, I wanted him to stay, but I was too exhausted to wake myself and tell him. I heard the lights go out in the kitchen, and then sleep overtook me.

Chapter Twelve

Addy

My head pounded when I woke the next morning. I felt the light hit my face and scrunched my eyes against it. I rolled over and opened one eye.

Fuck.

I'd fallen asleep with my contacts in.

Shit.

I swung my legs over the side of the bed and stumbled into the bathroom, still half asleep as I took my contact lenses out and threw them away. I made it back to my bed and found my glasses. When I slid them on, I saw a glass of water and some Advil on my nightstand. There was a sticky note next to the water.

I'm still here. I didn't leave. But I thought you might need these.

I felt tears at the edge of my eyes and blinked them away angrily. I took the Advil and downed the water. It was then I remembered I was still in that ridiculous dress. I sighed and found an old T-shirt and shorts and threw those on. I needed tea. Strong, black tea. Bitter enough to wash the regret out of my mouth and put some life back in my body.

I carefully made my way out of my room and down the hall, trying to keep my steps light.

I stopped in my tracks when I entered the living room. Asleep on my little couch was a bonafide demi-god. Somewhere in my exhausted brain was a dirty joke about tea not being the only thing that could make me feel alive.

He was shirtless, with one of his gigantic arms draped over his face, and my blanket over his lap. I cringed as I remembered crying into his shirt for hours, no doubt ruining it. I tip-toed into the kitchen and turned on the kettle, trying to be quiet, and apparently failing completely.

Bell stirred at the first noise I made and blinked sleepily at me.

"Good morning." His drawl was more pronounced in the morning, and it melted my insides.

"Morning," I said softly. "Would you like some tea? I'd offer coffee, but I don't drink it, so there's none in the house."

"Tea is fine. Whatever you're having, I'm not picky," he said, stretching his arms above his head as he stood.

My eyes dropped to his chest, and I bit my lip. My hazy brain was immediately sidetracked following the curves and dips of his muscles. Imagining all the things that man could do to me.

Now that I had allowed myself to be vulnerable, it seemed every wall I'd built for Bell was intent on crumbling down around me.

He snapped his fingers in front of my face, and I realized I'd spaced out fantasizing. I had the decency to blush and turned away quickly to get the cups down from the cupboard.

He kept his distance, leaning against the wall of the kitchen entrance, arms folded, watching me. No doubt cautious after last night's train wreck.

120

I had to admit that I liked that Bell didn't feel the need to force conversation. So many people would feel like they had to fill this increasingly tense silence with small talk. They seemed to think it made things more comfortable, when in reality it did the opposite.

But Bell simply watched me put water into the kettle, grab the tea from the drawer, and turn the burner on.

"My mom walked out on my dad and me when I was five," he said softly, breaking the silence.

I turned, confused. His eyes were on the ground. I realized that he was trying to make me feel better about last night by opening up to me in return.

I walked over to him and rested my hand on his forearm.

"You don't have to," I said, looking into his eyes so he knew I meant it.

He gave me a soft smile that was full of understanding and something else that I was terrified to give a name to. He covered my hand with his, holding me there, letting me know he wanted to share himself with me.

"She just left one day. Left for work and never came home. My dad said he tried to track her down, but the only thing he ever got was a packet of documents from a lawyer granting him full custody. My dad did the best he could, but I was five. I already wasn't an easy kid. All I knew was that one day I had a mom, and the next day I didn't. I thought it was all my fault. I thought that I hadn't been good enough for her to stay, you know?

"I hired a private investigator in college, and he found her. I reached out and she didn't even apologize. She just told me that it had been best for everyone, and that she didn't regret anything. She told me that if I wanted a relationship with her then I'd have to initiate everything. She'd never reach out to me, she wasn't going to try.

"She liked her life the way it was. I think she said, 'I'm not going to have my life interrupted by my past.' That shit took me years of therapy to work through. To finally realize that I wasn't the problem. That it had never been my fault that she'd left, that she hadn't wanted to be a mom anymore. I'd tried a few times to reach out to her after I found her, but eventually one of my therapists brought me to the realization that it was just rehashing old trauma every time I did, so I finally just stopped and focused on trying to heal."

I looked down at where our hands were resting. He'd laced our fingers together, and I liked how strong that made me feel.

"Thank you for telling me that."

"You said you needed to know someone," he shrugged. "I want you to know me, Addy. Everything, down to my soul. Because…"

He hesitated. He never hesitated. He always just came out and said what he meant. It was one of the things I liked most about him. I waited, but he seemed stuck.

"Because?"

"Dammit, Addy, because I want you to love me like I love you," he whispered.

That was the name for the look in his eyes. The one I'd been trying so hard not to think.

I dropped my hand, shocked. "You can't know you love me."

The denial sat heavy in my chest, because I knew that Bell probably did know me. He'd patiently coaxed information from me over the course of the past month or so, getting me to open up to him in a way that I hadn't with anyone. But love? That was getting into dangerous territory, and it scared the living daylights out of me.

He sighed heavily, his arms folding tighter over his chest.

"I know! It's crazy, but ever since that first kiss, that's all I can think about. And I don't trust it either. I'm clearly fucked up in my own ways, Addy, and I hate this shit.

"But for whatever reason, if it's really love or just some crazy intense connection we share, I can't walk away from you. I want to know you, truly and deeply, just like I know you want to know me."

I stared at him, my brain racing to put all of the pieces together. Then, I realized it would take more than just a few seconds to do that.

I blinked a few times, and then turned to look at my calendar on my fridge. It was Saturday, so I was free and clear, but he owned a restaurant. His schedule had to be different from most peoples'.

"Do you have work today?" I asked him over my shoulder.

"What?" He was clearly confused at the leap my brain had taken.

I turned to him and took his hands in mine.

"Stay with me today, and we can learn all about each other," I said softly. "I'll tell you anything you want to know, as long as you promise to do the same. Spend the day with me."

His eyes shone as he beamed down at me. My own personal sun god.

"Deal."

***

We were lounging on the floor, a pile of blankets surrounding us. We hadn't ever gotten out of our pajamas. My hair was still a mess, Bell still didn't have a shirt on, but I was happier than I'd been in a long time. We had spent the morning trading stories.

We'd gone a bit more in depth of my feelings surrounding the hospital stay, and why I'd chosen MMA after that. I had never wanted to feel so powerless ever again. MMA was the perfect choice because it showed me how to step into my power. It was also something that I could use for everyday self-defense without having to think too much about it. It was hard to feel vulnerable and powerless when I knew that I could incapacitate most people with one kick and no remorse.

He'd gone into detail about the plethora of therapists he'd been through, citing a pretty valid reason for leaving each one before finally landing on one he trusted. He still saw her once a month. I told him all about Dr. Laura, and how she'd been the perfect person to help me through everything that had happened. I told him how supportive she had been of him since the beginning.

He told me his favorite color (purple, same as mine), his favorite food (his grandma's mac and cheese casserole), his favorite singer (Frank Sinatra), and his favorite hiking spot (Cloudland Canyon State Park, a few hours north of us).

He asked me about my favorite movies (any of the Fast and Furious, but also the eight-hour Pride and Prejudice with Colin Firth), my ultimate goal in life (to own a few acres of property and keep bees), and my go to place to be alone (the beach, any beach).

I'd told him my middle and last name (Adelaide Doris Jones, I was still miffed with my parents about that one). He'd explained how Bell had come to be his nickname.

He was born Jackson Reed Hawthorne but had climbed up to the bell tower at his church as a boy and decided to ring it with his head. The nickname stuck after that.

I had tested out Jackson, and decided that while I liked it for him, Bell suited him better.

He had asked me about my aversion to coffee (he was an addict), and I'd told him. I had never been a coffee drinker. When Derek and I went on our first date, it was to a coffee shop, and he made fun of me for not liking coffee. He'd insisted he could find a coffee concoction that I would like and had refused to take no for an answer. He'd bought me some frothy thing, and I hadn't wanted to disappoint him, so I'd pretended to enjoy it. After that, he would only buy me that particular drink. Through our entire relationship, I'd drank coffee even though I'd hated it. I had later realized that was just one of the ways that he'd controlled me. I could barely stomach the smell of it now.

We'd laughed, we'd been serious. I'd only cried a little bit. It was now late afternoon, and the sun was slanting through the blinds, casting shadows.

I'd made us some sandwiches and was settling back down next to him when I noticed he was looking at me strangely.

"What's that look for?" I asked, my voice light.

"What's the weirdest thing about you? Like, a weird habit, or nervous tick? Something you've never told anyone else." He was deadly serious.

I took a bite of my sandwich and thought about that. I knew the answer immediately, I was just hesitant to tell him. But we'd shared so much today, and I'd told him I would be honest.

"I like to go places by myself," I finally admitted. "Especially natural places – hikes, forests, rivers, stuff like that."

"That's not that weird," he pursed his lips.

I laughed. "No, that part isn't. But this next part is, if you don't get it, and a lot of people don't. I like to go to these places by myself, and to isolate myself in them because I can hear them. I can hear the earth whispering, and I can feel the wisdom of the trees and the rocks. I can feel their energy, and it's very calming to me. But if I'm with someone, they don't talk to me. I've always felt special, like the planet trusts me enough to tell me some of her secrets."

He was quiet for a moment, contemplating me. I knew he must think I was crazy. I sometimes did. But this connection with nature had pulled me through some of the worst moments since the attack.

125

It's why running had become to therapeutic for me. Being outside, giving all of my stress and worry and fears to the air and the earth, grounded me.

It brought me back to my center. To the person that I'd been before the attack. Someone who loved deeply and wasn't afraid. I don't know how he'd known how to ask that question, but it had been a good one.

I squirmed a bit under his gaze, hoping that hadn't been the revelation that would scare him off. Finally, he reached over and pulled me closer to him. His breath fanned across my face, and my heart stuttered.

"I don't think that's weird, Addy. I think it's beautiful," he said softly. His finger came up and traced down my cheek. "I think you're beautiful."

I couldn't breathe. He was looking at me with such adoration. My eyes widened in panic, and he pressed his lips to my cheek.

"Don't run away from me, Addy," he pleaded. "Trust that whatever you're seeing in my face that's scaring you is real. And trust that I'm not going anywhere."

My fight or flight had kicked in, and he was right. All I wanted to do was run away. Instead, I closed my eyes and took a few deep breaths. When I opened them, he was watching me cautiously. I bit my lip, hesitant to trust the way he was looking at me.

I had to get closer.

I lifted myself onto my knees and swung one leg over him, so that I was straddling his lap. I reached up slowly to cradle his face. I let my fingers sweep over his high cheekbones, flutter over his beautiful lips, and trail down his neck.

He never took his eyes off me as I explored, searching for any sign of dishonesty. But he was so open, so relaxed. His hands rested on my thighs, and he made no sudden movements. He simply let me explore.

My hands made their way down his neck, over his broad shoulders, and down his arms. I grabbed his hands and placed them on my lower back, prompting him to pull me closer. I needed to be closer to him.

I rested my forehead against his. Time stopped as we breathed each other in.

"I don't want to run away from you," I whispered, my heart beating loudly in my chest.

"I don't want you to run away."

I took a deep breath. "I don't want to be friends, either."

He stilled and pulled his face away, looking confused and hurt.

I realized too late how I should have modified that statement. I always messed up with words. They never came out right.

How do I fix this? How could I tell him what I really meant? That I wanted him, in every meaning of the word?

His eyes searched my face, and then he started leaning away from me. No! He had to stay close!

I grabbed his face in my hands and brought our lips together. Probably a little too forcefully, but I was desperate for him to understand.

He froze for half a second before the alchemy between us kicked in and his hands were on my ass, pulling me into his body.

His mouth ravaged mine, his tongue sweeping through my open mouth possessively. I gave as good as I got, biting his lip gently and coming back for more.

His lips dropped to my neck and he pressed open mouthed kisses to the delicate skin there. I arched against him as my head went back, giving him better access.

Heat flooded my body, and suddenly I was rocking slightly on his lap. I felt him harden beneath me, and I knew Raelynn had been right.

He was huge.

He nipped my collarbone, and a low moan escaped my throat. His face pulled back, and our eyes met. Electricity sparked between us, and I could feel his heartbeat under my palm, racing just like mine was.

His eyes were lost, his pupils blown, and his breathing was ragged. I was soaked, just from a little making out. I couldn't imagine what it would be like to be naked and at his disposal.

I felt like a raw nerve. Nobody had ever known me so deeply. Nobody had ever made me feel so safe with them. I had never wanted to give myself to someone so badly.

I leaned down and pressed a soft kiss to his lips, trying desperately not to move too much.

This was going too fast. Moving too quickly.

I'd been in this situation before. And Derek hadn't stopped me. We'd fucked each other senseless by our second date.

"Hey," Bell's rough, honeysuckle voice interrupted my panicking.

I looked at him and he wiped a tear from the corner of my eye.

"Addy," he breathed, his voice laced with awe and warmth. "Darling, we don't have to do anything you're not comfortable with. We can spend the next year of our lives staying six feet away from each other, if that's what you want."

He was trying to make me laugh, and it worked. A small chuckle left me, and I dropped my head against his chest.

"You feel it too, though, right?" I whispered, suddenly self-conscious. I mean, I had basically mauled him. What if he didn't feel the connection like I did?

"Adelaide," he said my name like a prayer. "I would make love to you on every surface of this house, several times, and still never want to let you go. You can't know what you're doing to me, sitting on me like this. It's taking every bit of self-control I have not to tear your clothes off and eat you for lunch instead of that sandwich."

I'm not sure if it was the reassurance that he wanted me as much as I wanted him, or if it was the sincerity of his tone, but I suddenly realized that this was part of trusting him. That I'd trusted him with my past and he'd stayed. I wanted to trust him with my body now, too.

"Bell," I said softly. I lifted my eyes to his and then placed a gentle kiss on his lips. "We need to slow down. But there is something that I've been dying to do, pretty much since our first conversation."

I slowly slid myself down his body. I settled between his legs, and looked up at him, waiting for him to tell me no. His eyes were wide, and his tongue danced across his lip.

I tapped his hip and he lifted so that I could pull his pants down.

He was still half-hard from our make-out session, but even half was more than I'd ever seen.

I took him in my hand and gently stroked, amazed at the way he fit perfectly in my grip. He probably had the most perfect penis I'd ever seen. It was like it had been tailor-made for my hand.

His breath hitched, and when we made eye contact, he stiffened further in my hand.

A wicked smile flashed across my face as I lowered my mouth, holding his gaze the whole time.

My tongue flicked out and I lapped up the bead of salt that had been leaking. I'd never cared much for the taste of men before, but Bell was different. It made me moan, and my eyes fluttered closed.

His dick jumped in my hand, and I gave it another pump.

This was something I was good at. Something I really enjoyed. I could feel how wet I was just from this simple act.

I opened my eyes and, holding his gaze, took him all the way down my throat in one smooth, slow motion.

Then I swallowed.

His hips thrust forward and his head fell back. He let out the most perfect growl I had ever heard.

"Fuck, Addy, just like that," he moaned.

I grabbed his hand and twisted it in my hair. I wanted him to take what he needed. He'd been so patient, so kind, so understanding. I needed to give him this. I bobbed up and down on his shaft, my tongue pressed firmly on the large vein running up the underside. When I'd get to the top, I let my hand do a little twist before sinking back down onto it.

Feeling his cock stretching my mouth made me vibrate with need.

I reached my other hand down and cradled his balls.

It took some coaxing, but after a few minutes he was thrusting into my mouth, his head thrown back.

I hummed to show my approval and was rewarded with a rush of precum. I swallowed it down greedily.

"Addy, you need to stop, I'm going to come any second here," his voice was tight.

I answered by impaling my throat on his cock and tugging his balls at the same time.

His head flew forward and we made eye contact as I swallowed around him one more time, and then he was coming.

He blew down my throat and I swallowed it all. He tasted salty, but not unpleasant. I licked him up and down gently, cleaning him up. And then placed a gentle kiss on the tip of his dick.

He reached down and grabbed me, pulling me back up to straddle his lap before kissing me. He moaned when he tasted himself there.

130

"Adelaide Jones, you are something else," he whispered.

"I wanted to thank you, for everything you've done for me since we met," I muttered against his lips.

"And how can I ever thank you?" His drawl sent fire down to my core.

I smirked. "There's no need."

"Addy," he said sternly. "I am, first and foremost, a gentleman."

His arms cradled my back as he laid me down on the blankets. His hands were soft as they trailed down my body, his fingers catching the hem of my shorts. He stopped, watching me. The rise and fall of my chest as I struggled to breathe, my eyes fluttering from his touch.

"Please," I choked out. I was so turned on that I was going to come in seconds. I knew that, but I needed it.

He pulled my shorts off in one swift movement and spread my legs. My knees touched the floor and he groaned.

"God, you're so fucking perfect," he whispered.

Before I could answer, his tongue was on me.

"You're so wet," he moaned. "You liked that just as much as I did, didn't you?"

"Maybe more," I joked.

His tongue swept a long stripe up my lips, and then flicked at my clit. I was so wound up that my whole body shuddered.

"Please, Bell," I moaned, my fingers twisting in the blankets as I tried to hold it off.

I felt his smirk as two fingers sank inside me, his tongue swirling around me. He crooked his fingers, pumped, and sucked hard, and I was soaring.

My stomach clenched as the heat that had been building inside me since the day we met came to a crescendo. Every muscle in my body tensed as he worked me, and with one more hard suck I was falling. I could feel my legs shaking, my body writhing on the ground as my orgasm washed over me.

Bell moaned as he licked me up, tasting my come on his lips. His fingers pumped slowly as he brought me back down to reality.

Finally, my head stopped spinning, and I looked up at this perfect man who was leaning over me, peppering my chest with kisses.

"Much better than six feet apart, wasn't it?" I said breathlessly.

He laughed and kissed me softly.

"I adore you, Adelaide Jones."

Chapter Thirteen

Bell

If I'd thought I was obsessed before, it was nothing compared to now. I'd had a taste of having her, the most perfect woman on the face of the earth, and she'd become all I could think about.

After spending the entire weekend together, I was loathe to let her go to work, but she insisted on maintaining boundaries, one of which was that we needed to spend time apart.

I knew she was right. We couldn't rush this just because we'd made a monumental leap in our relationship. She was still healing, I was still working through my own doubts and fears. We needed to keep it slow.

Knowing that didn't stop me from texting her as much as I could, calling her when I knew she'd be free, and talking about her almost constantly to Greg.

That's what I was doing when he actually slapped a hand over my mouth.

"Bud, you've got to get a grip," he said with a forced chuckle. "I get it, the girl's the best thing since the motor engine, but we're trying to start a staff meeting."

He gestured to the room full of our staff, who were watching us curiously. We'd been alone just a few moments before, and I guess I'd been so caught up talking about Addy that I hadn't heard everybody come in.

I cleared my throat and thanked the good Lord for my dark skin to hide the heat in my cheeks.

"Right, let's get started then," I said seriously.

***

I was sweating bullets as I pulled up outside of Addy's apartment and parked.

Tonight was our first official date, with all the romantic bells and whistles. I was taking her dancing, but she didn't know that. I'd just told her to wear something sexy and to be ready at seven.

I rode the elevator up and knocked once on the door.

I heard a muffled curse and something fall over and had to hide my smile as the door flew open.

An angel was standing in front of me, hopping on one foot while trying to squeeze her other into a heel that made her legs look like sex.

I instinctively reached out a hand to steady her and she gripped my arm roughly, but I didn't miss the slight flinch of her body away from mine.

She smiled gratefully at me as she slipped the shoe on and stood on both feet. I took the hand holding her and spun her around so I could take her in.

She was wearing the blue dress she'd been wearing last Friday night when she'd sat down at my bar. I hadn't really looked at it then, because I was trying to be a good friend, but now... my eyes raked over the revealing cut that showed the curve of her full breasts, the skirt that flirted with her strong thighs, the heels that lifted her to the perfect height for leaning her head against my shoulder while we were dancing. My tongue snaked over my lips and I watched her pupils blow wide as her breathing hitched.

I gently pulled her towards me and lowered my lips to hers. I hesitated, wanting her to know that until she gave me permission she was completely in charge.

A small growl rumbled from her throat, and before I could be shocked her lips were attacking mine. Her hands clasped behind my neck and she pressed her body fully against mine. My hands gripped her hips and I ground my growing erection into her stomach as I explored her mouth.

This woman could get me going with a single look, but the sounds she was making as we kissed were almost my undoing. I pulled back, panting, to look into her lust blown eyes. A small, disbelieving chuckle escaped me, and I rested my forehead on hers.

Since the physical barrier had come down between us Addy had been ravenous. I couldn't lie, I knew exactly how she felt. It took every ounce of self-control I had in me not to take her in my arms and never let her go.

"Hello to you too," I said. My voice was rough with desire, and an actual shiver ran down her body.

I took a deep breath and leaned back.

"C'mon, we've got reservations," I grinned.

She patted her dress nervously and grabbed her keys and purse. She locked the triple deadbolt on the door and then turned to me with an expectant grin.

"Where are we going?" she asked. She was excited and she wasn't hiding it. I fell a little harder.

"Dancing," I winked. "Let's go."

***

We'd agreed that we wouldn't do sleepovers for at least a few weeks, but damn if leaving her at her door at the end of the night wasn't the hardest thing I'd ever done.

After having her body pressed against mine all night as I'd whispered in her ear everything I'd like to do to her, I was beyond worked up. I'd need a long shower when I got home, but it was totally worth it.

Addy looked up at me from the doorway. We'd been saying goodbye for half an hour, and I knew that eventually I would have to leave.

"Can I ask you something?" she said timidly.

I brushed a curl out of her face and traced my thumb down her cheek. "You can ask me anything, anytime, anywhere."

"How'd you get so good at this dating thing?"

I blinked. "You think I did a good job?"

She laughed, not believing me. "Of course you did. Dancing, drinks, romance, fun. It was the perfect first date."

I shook my head and smiled to myself. "I haven't actually ever really dated anyone. I was always scared that if I got close to someone they'd leave, so I kept things casual. This is the first time I've ever tried to plan a date, so I'm glad I did well."

Her eyes were soft and glowing as she looked at me. Then she pushed up on her tiptoes and kissed my cheek.

"You did perfect. And I'm glad I'm your first real date."

I hooked my arm around her and pressed our lips together tenderly. "Me too, darlin'. Me too."

When I got home, I let myself really think about the last time I'd gone to any effort for a date. It was a long time ago, if ever.

Panic rose up in me. I was so scared I was going to screw this up. That she was going to leave. That I wouldn't be good enough for her. I had my therapist's voice in my head telling me the logical thoughts – that I needed to try in order to find out. That even if we weren't forever I'd be okay, because I've always been okay. But I also realized that…maybe I wanted this to be forever.

I'd known for weeks now that I couldn't imagine a life without Addy in it. Without her warmth. Without her arms wrapped around me. Without her smile. I didn't know if I wanted to exist in a world where I didn't have those things. But this was the first time that it occurred to me that this could be it.

This could be the last first date I ever went on. She could be my last first kiss. And I knew that I wanted her to be my last first everything for the rest of my life.

I blew out a breath through my nose as I fell back onto my bed.

I needed to keep these thoughts to myself. I didn't want to scare her off when she wanted to go slow.

But I knew. I wanted her. For as long as she'd let me have her.

Chapter Fourteen

Addy

Bell: Good morning, gorgeous.

Bell's text chimed through, waking me from the state of half sleep I was in.

He always made sure to let me know he was thinking of me. He checked in a few times a day, just wanting to know how my day was going, how I was feeling, if I needed anything. When I had asked him why he did this he'd grinned like the Devil and kissed me senseless.

"If I can't do that at least every few hours, then I just have to settle for knowing you're thinking of me, don't I?" he'd said. His eyes had glittered and he looked at me like I was his whole world.

He terrified me.

And I was so, so happy.

***

It had been six weeks since we'd sat in my living room telling our life stories to each other. Every day I learned more about him.

And every day I was able to open up more to the idea of him. Of trusting how he felt about me.

Laura was a huge help in this. Every time we made a step forward, I made sure to walk through all of the implications with her. I just wanted to be sure that I wouldn't freak out if Bell did something that triggered me, and there were times that just being in a relationship was hard for me to accept. But over time I was slowly starting to actually believe that Bell's feelings were real. He knew more about me than anyone ever had, and he still wanted to be with me. It was a feeling that I could get high on for the rest of my life.

I clocked out of work and slung my sweater over my arm as I stood to leave. I waved goodbye to the girls and made my way to the door.

The sun was low in the sky, and its warmth made me smile softly as it touched my face. It reminded me of the feel of Bell's fingers when they traced my jawline.

I sighed happily and opened my eyes. They landed on a rusted old Camaro parked across the street. I cocked my head and tried to figure out why I was suddenly uneasy. I had seen the car around before. Not very often, but a few times a month. But the longer I stared at it, the more I felt like it was watching me back.

Then, my phone buzzed in my pocket, making me jump.

A smile flitted across my face when I saw the caller ID. All of my unease melted away.

"Hello, handsome," I smirked into the phone.

"Hello, gorgeous," his silky drawl answered, but there was something off in his tone.

"Everything okay?" I asked softly.

"I need to see you," his voice was rough.

"Well, lucky for you I just got off work," I said, trying to lighten the mood.

"Perfect," he nearly growled down the line. "Can I come over?"

"Now?"

"I told you, I need you," he breathed. He almost sounded…insecure? Scared? I couldn't quite put my finger on it.

My smile faded a bit. This was different. I'd never heard him like this before.

"Okay, yeah, of course, Bell," I said solemnly. "Come over. I'll meet you at my place."

***

Bell was waiting on the front stoop of my apartment when I got off the bus. It dropped me right in front of my building, and I could see my apartment from the stop. Bell was sitting with his head in his hands. He lifted his gaze to me as I approached him carefully. His eyes were tinged red, like he'd been crying. I placed a hand softly on his cheek, and he lifted his eyes to mine. They were haunted. I wrapped my arms around him and he clung to me. I felt a hot tear drop onto my skin.

"Let's go inside," I whispered.

Once we were in my apartment, he settled himself on the couch. I grabbed us some drinks and went to sit beside him, but he pulled me into his lap and held me. For a long time, we just sat there, breathing in each other's presence. I felt him start and stop the same sentence a few times before growling softly.

"You don't have to talk about it," I said softly, my finger tracing abstract patterns along his chest.

He let out a heavy sigh, and then placed a kiss on my temple, but didn't say anything.

"I'll make us some food, yeah?" I offered, standing.

He followed me into the kitchen, hovering close. He stood near me, touching me when he could, as I made us some quesadillas on the stove. We ate silently at the counter, his hand holding mine. He still hadn't spoken, and I was trying not to worry. After the food was gone, I simply watched him for a moment before pulling him into me for another long embrace.

His arms tightened around me and I felt a tension release in his shoulders. And then he was crying. I held him as he sobbed into my neck, his face buried. I'd never seen a grown man actually cry. It was heartbreaking, and I was touched that Bell trusted me enough to feel his real feelings around me.

After a few moments he straightened and trained his eyes on the ground. I watched him carefully, and then led him to the couch.

We sat and I curled myself into his lap, my arms wrapped around his waist. He placed a soft kiss on my forehead.

I don't know how long we sat like that, not speaking, just being with each other. I watched the shadows grow on the walls, and the sky outside darkened. Bell never fully relaxed, but I didn't want to pressure him to tell me what was going on. I could tell that he just needed me to be there with him, and that he would tell me in time.

When the clock chimed eight, he let out a heavy sigh, and dropped his head to mine.

"My mom died," he finally whispered.

I blinked up at him, not knowing what to say.

"What happened?" I finally asked.

He took a deep breath and ran a hand down his face.

"Hit and run, I guess," he sighed. "She died instantly. They caught the driver a few streets down. There were a lot of witnesses, and his car was wrecked. He's in jail."

"Oh, Bell," I whispered, tightening my arms around him. I didn't know what else to say.

"She left me her house."

"Really?"

"Yeah. I guess she never had any other children, and she never remarried, and she didn't want any of her family to have it, so she left it to me. Her lawyer said that she'd amended her will when she bought the house twenty years ago to leave it to me. Sole ownership."

Wow. I wasn't sure how to process this, but I took a moment and realized it wasn't about me. I looked up at him and touched his cheek gently. "So, she never really forgot about you."

"I guess not."

Silence fell over the room again.

"Is there anything I can do for you, to help you through this?" I asked softly, my fingers tracing his jawline.

A sweet smile flickered across his face but didn't reach his eyes. "I just want to hold you."

I grinned. "That we can do."

Chapter Fifteen

Addy

Funerals weren't my thing. Not that they were anyone's favorite thing. Anything remotely emotionally taxing was definitely outside of my comfort zone. But Bell had asked me to come, so there I was.

There weren't a lot of people in the small church. There was a photo of Bell's mother. She was beautiful. I saw her high cheekbones and sharp jawline reflected on Bell's face. But everything else about Bell was his father.

I hadn't thought Bell's father would be at the funeral, but when I'd looked a little confused upon the introduction he'd just laughed and said that he'd forgiven his ex-wife a long time ago, and that celebrating her life was the least he could do for the gift she'd given him of Bell.

Marlon was everything good about the world. He was charming, sweet, handsome, and just so kind. Every good quality of Bell's was magnified in his father. They were clearly very close. Bell's eyes lit up when he talked with his dad, and he'd been so nervous to introduce me.

"Bellboy here's never brought a girl to meet me before," Marlon had teased, his eyes twinkling.

"Well, they must not have been special enough," I joked.

Marlon had laughed lightly but looked at me with a gravity that made me realize I'd hit the nail on the head.

I was special to Bell. He'd told me that he'd never done the relationship thing before, but to also know that I was the only girl he'd ever introduced to his father? Something shifted in my perception of our relationship then. It was like it cemented that I was just as important to Bell as he was to me. It was comforting. And terrifying.

I'd held Bell's hand throughout the whole ceremony, and as the casket had been lowered into the ground. He didn't let go throughout dinner with his dad, or the car ride home. He didn't let go as he crawled into bed and rested his head on my chest. And when we woke up in the morning our hands were still entwined.

***

I woke to a warm feeling growing in my core. I wiggled a bit, and two strong hands gripped my hips, holding me in place. I felt a long, strong tongue sweep up my center, and I shuddered as I fully woke up.

I looked down to find Bell grinning as he lapped leisurely at my core. He started with long strokes from the bottom and flicked at that beautiful bundle of nerves when he got to the top.

Holy fuck.

I whimpered as I tried to grind myself onto his lips, but his strong grip kept me from moving. I still tried and was reprimanded with a sharp nip to my inner thigh.

"Today, you're mine," he growled. His voice was husky from sleep, and his drawl was exaggerated from his arousal.

"Fuck, Bell, keep talking like that and I won't need your

tongue," I gasped.

A devilish grin split his face, and then he devoured me.

My head thrashed back as the coil tightened in my stomach. I moaned as his long tongue pierced in and out of me. And then it was circling my clit, and two of his fingers were inside of me. Pumping me.

"Bell," I warned.

"I want it all, darlin'," he growled, and then bit down and pumped his fingers hard.

My whole body shuddered with my release, and he moaned as he lapped it all up.

He loved waking me up like this, and it was my favorite way to wake up, if I was being honest.

When we'd first talked about it, I'd been apprehensive, mainly because I didn't know how my half-conscious mind would react to feeling his body on mine as I was waking up. But the groundwork of trust and communication that we'd built had proved to be helpful in all aspects of our relationship. There was never a moment that I didn't trust Bell with every part of me.

As my heart rate slowed, he climbed up my body and took my lips in his. I moaned when I tasted myself on him, and he smiled against me.

"Good morning, beautiful," he whispered.

I grinned up at him. I wrapped my left leg around his waist, brought my right foot flat against the bed, placed my right hand on his shoulder, and in one swift move flipped us so that I was straddling his lap and he was staring at me, dazed.

"You've been holding out on me, Addy." His voice was rough, and I could feel his hardness beneath me.

"MMA comes in handy in the bedroom, too," I giggled.

His eyes widened in excitement as I lowered myself down his

body, more than ready to return the favor.

***

I was five minutes late to my appointment with Dr. Laura and I was frustrated with myself because there was a lot I needed to cover today. So, when my butt hit the chair, I launched into it with no preamble.

Bell had been spending every night with me since he'd gotten the news of his mom's passing. We'd completely broken our no sleepovers rule, and I wasn't actually that upset about it.

It felt like a new milestone in our relationship. Especially after we'd gone to her funeral together. That was an event that would cement me in his memory. It was a big deal for me.

This whole relationship was a big deal for me. And I was considering asking him if he wanted to move in together. I knew that it would have to be a conversation, considering how quickly I'd moved in with Derek. It made me a bit gun-shy, but the fact that I was contemplating it was a huge breakthrough for me.

We'd not been dating that long, just a few months, but I knew everything about Bell. I'd been completely honest with him about everything in my past, and he hadn't run away. He also hadn't pressured me to do anything physically that I didn't want to do.

Bell was so different from anyone I'd ever dated. Yes, there had been the initial physical attraction, but even before that Bell had made me feel safe. He'd protected me from that asshole in the bar. He didn't even know me, but he stood up for me because he's a genuinely good person.

And when I examined this a little further, I'd realized that "safe" was really the core of our relationship. I felt safe with him, and he felt safe with me. We shared everything with each other. He excited me, of course, but there was also this sense of steady, constant security.

"It sounds like you've come a long way with Bell," Laura said as the hour came to a close.

"I have," I sighed happily. "I think I lo-"

All of the air seemed to leave the room. My eyes locked with Laura's, who didn't look surprised. Instead, she had a small, expectant smile on her face.

"Not saying something gives it more power than it deserves," she reminded me softly.

I swallowed around the hard lump in my throat as my eyes stung. "I love him?"

"Do you?"

"I – I mean," I blew out a sigh. "He makes me happier than I ever thought I could be. He makes me feel safe. He protects me. He supports and encourages me. And I think about him all the time. My chest hurts when I'm not with him, and when we *are* together I feel... settled."

"And do you think that's love?"

"Isn't it? It's the exact opposite of the way that Derek made me feel. I thought I'd loved Derek. But I know that that wasn't real love. What if this is?"

Laura leaned forward, her warm eyes drilling into mine. "Do you think it is?"

I thought about the way that it felt waking up next to Bell, like a ball of light was living in my core. I thought about how I never wanted that feeling to go away.

"I want to believe that this is love," I whispered.

Laura sat back, a huge grin on her face. "Then it is."

I sat back as well, my heart hammering in my chest. This was an unprecedented revelation for me, and I wanted to shout from the window that I was in love.

"I want to tell everyone," I laughed, my cheeks heating.

"I think there's someone that should be the first to know," Laura laughed with me.

She was right. And the more I thought about it, the more I knew exactly how I wanted to tell him.

***

The Bell Tower was packed. It was Friday night, and the jazz band was in full swing. Couples were dancing, the restaurant was filled with laughter and warmth. It was the perfect atmosphere for a date night.

Bell led the way to a private table in the far corner of the room. Whenever we came here, Bell had the staff set up this table with a few ferns separating it from the rest of the restaurant. We could still look out over the dining area and watch people as they went about their evenings, but there was a bit more privacy than being in the main space. It was perfect.

The waitress brought over a bottle of the night's specialty draft, and our usual starters.

Bell thanked her and then his gaze fell to my face. His eyes watched me as if mesmerized.

"What?" I asked, tucking a strand of hair behind my ear.

"You're just…gorgeous. Inside and out."

I blushed and leaned over to kiss him. Our lips met slowly, and the room disappeared. The music stopped, the chatter died, the lights dimmed. It was just us in that moment.

I leaned back and found myself suddenly nervous. Then the band started up a new song, and I recognized it as the one the older couple had danced to on my first time here.

148

"Let's dance!" I said, standing and pulling him over to the dance floor with me.

He laughed his deep belly laugh that filled my body with warmth from head to toe and swept me into his arms. We swayed softly to the music, and I leaned my head on his chest.

This was it. The perfect moment.

I looked up at him and stole a kiss. He smiled down at me, looking at me like I was his entire world.

"Bell," I said, linking my arms around his neck.

"Yes, my darlin'?" he teased, pulling me somehow closer.

I watched his face, unable to take my eyes from his.

"I love you."

He blinked once. Then twice. His jaw fell slack, and his mouth formed a perfect O as he processed what I'd said. It took him a moment, and I was internally panicking.

We'd stopped moving, and were just looking at each other, when suddenly his eyes sparkled and his face split into the biggest smile I'd ever seen.

He lifted me off my feet, held me high above him, and twirled me around, laughing all the while.

As he set me down, his hand tangled in the back of my hair and he kissed the breath right out of my lungs.

When we pulled away, I laughed softly and watched him.

"Oh, Addy," he said adoringly, "I love you too."

I felt my eyes well with tears. I was so happy. My heart hammered in my chest, and if I could have lifted him off his feet I would have.

He smiled and leaned down to pepper my face with kisses, muttering, "I love you" after each and every one. And I believed him.

***

We crashed through the door to my apartment, our laughter building as we struggled to keep our hands off of each other.

Our evening had been lighthearted and carefree since our moment on the dance floor. Nothing else in the world mattered except Bell. We'd drank, we'd danced more, we'd laughed the entire night.

The energy shifted as soon as the lock on the front door clicked. I turned and saw Bell leaning against the kitchen wall, his suit jacket over his arm, watching me sweetly.

I grinned to myself. I wanted tonight to be perfect, and I had planned exactly how our night would end.

I tilted my head to one side as I contemplated him. His face turned worried, and then confused, as I slowly approached him.

I ran my hand up his arm, and then down his chest, watching as his breathing hitched and he tried to control himself. I snaked my arm around his waist and placed a soft kiss on his chest. When I looked up at him, I saw his eyes flash with desire. My favorite look.

I smirked, and then took a step back. His eyes softened, and it was his turn to cock his head.

As he watched me, I slowly slid one of the straps of my dress down my arm. His tongue flicked out over his lip. I slid the other strap down, and then stepped into his space and turned around.

"Can you unzip me?" I asked, my voice low.

I threw a glance over my shoulder and saw that his eyes were watching me carefully. He was calculating the energy shift, trying to figure out what I wanted. He slowly dragged the zipper down my back.

I let the dress fall to the floor and stood in front of him in a lacy black bra and panty set, and my stilettos.

I watched his Adam's apple bob as his eyes drifted down my body. Sauntering over to the hallway, knowing he was watching my every move, I had never felt so sexy, so wanted. So safe. I looked back and gave him my best 'come and get me' look, and then disappeared into the bedroom.

I heard his soft footsteps coming down the hall, but I didn't turn around. I made my way to the bed, and settled on the end, crossing my legs.

When I looked up, Bell was leaning against the doorframe, watching me. His shirtsleeves were rolled up to his elbows, and his arms were crossed, pulling the fabric of his shirt taught over his chest. I let my eyes trail across his broad shoulders. His pulse raced in his neck, giving away that he was just as excited as I was, even though his demeanor was frustratingly calm.

My eyes finally found his face, and when I saw the look in his eyes, desire settled deep in my core. He looked like he wanted to devour me.

He watched me for a moment, his eyes drawn to the rise and fall of my chest. Then our eyes met again, and a slow smile spread across his face.

"Tell me what you want, Addy," his voice was low, gravelly. Powerful.

A shiver ran down my spine. "You."

He tutted and shook his head, taking a few steps closer to me.

"I need you to be specific, Adelaide. Tell me what you *want*."

I swallowed around the lump in my throat, my heart pounding. This was quickly getting out of my control. I'd never heard him talk like this. He was usually so gentle and laid back, but this?

This was demanding. This was authoritative. This was dominant. And everything inside of me was telling me to submit. Every nerve in my body wanted to. Instead of being scared of losing control, I was excited to give it to him.

"I want you inside of me," I breathed. "I want to feel all of you. I want you to claim me. I want you to show me how much you love me."

His eyes flashed, and then he was standing in front of me.

"Lay back, sweetheart," his voice was soft, and I couldn't have stopped myself if I'd tried.

My back hit the mattress and my heart rate skyrocketed. As he towered over me, he held my gaze as he slowly loosened his tie with one hand, and threw his jacket onto the ground with the other. I watched him toe off his shoes and kneel gently on the end of the bed.

His eyes raked over my body and I wanted to squirm under his gaze.

"Don't move unless I tell you to," he ordered.

I swallowed around the arousal in my throat and managed to stop myself from nodding. His lips split in a wicked grin and he lifted one of my legs, kissing my ankle softly.

"What a good girl you are, Addy." The roughness in his voice sent a twinge right to my core.

"Bell," I whined, my body aching to move.

"I want this to be perfect for you," he smiled as he kissed his way up my leg, using his strong hand to push the other one open. "Look at you, so beautiful, so wet, just for me."

"Yes," I gasped. "It's all for you."

He growled into my center and the vibration made my hips thrust. His hands were lightning fast as they gripped my hips and pinned them to the mattress.

"What did I say about moving?" he whispered. "Am I going to have to tie you down?"

"God, please yes,." My brain short-circuited.

He chuckled to himself as his teeth gripped the lace thong and slid it down my legs. Then he was back and licked a stripe up my lips.

"Another time, maybe. Right now, I want to watch you try not to move as I make you come with my tongue."

I didn't have time to process what he'd said before he had buried his face between my legs and was licking me up like his last meal.

This wasn't anything new to us, but every time he took me with his mouth it was like the first time. He worshiped my body, drawing out every sound he could from me while his hands kept me firmly on the bed.

When I finally shattered, he hummed approvingly and kissed his way up my body. When he got to the black bra he buried his face between my breasts, inhaling like I was his favorite smell. Maybe I was. His hands roughly pulled my bra down and he took a nipple in his mouth and bit down, causing an embarrassing mewl to escape from my mouth.

"Addy, make that noise again."

He shuddered and then bit my other nipple. It wasn't the exact same sound, but it must have been close enough because he groaned against me.

"Please, Bell, I need you inside of me," I panted. Between his teeth on one breast, his fingers on the other, and the bulge in his pants rubbing against my leg I was about to come undone again.

"Do you think you could come just from this?" he rumbled against my chest.

I couldn't answer, but my breath caught as my hips ground against his body.

Suddenly, my wrists were in his hands and he had pinned them above my head as he hovered over me. He paused as his eyes searched my face.

His grip on my wrists wasn't tight, but I knew he was checking to make sure I was okay with being restrained. We looked deep into each other's eyes for a long moment, my chest heaving. I gave him a small nod, which earned me a mischievous smile from the god above me. Then, the smile disappeared and he looked at me seriously.

"Did I tell you to move?" His eyes were black, and I bit my lip to keep from saying something sarcastic.

Instead, I shook my head. "No, you didn't."

He leaned down and nipped at my neck.

"No, I didn't."

His tongue traced its way up to my ear, and his breath was hot as he whispered, "What am I going to do with you, Adelaide Jones?"

"Fuck me, please." The plea came from the depths of my soul. "I need to feel you inside of me, right now, or I might explode."

"Gorgeous, you'll be exploding either way," he laughed, and then sat up to unbutton his pants and slide them off.

As he worked his briefs off, I slid my hand under the pillow and pulled out a condom. Surprise flitted across his face.

"You planned all of this, didn't you?"

I smiled playfully at him. "I knew I wouldn't be able to stop myself once I'd told you I loved you. Thought I should be prepared."

He snatched the condom from me and ripped it open with his teeth, then he held the packet out to me.

"Put it on me."

His tone left no room for debate, but I arched an eyebrow.

"Does this mean I can move?"

"You'd better," he laughed softly to himself as I took him in my hands.

He felt so good in my grip, so hard, and my body trembled at the thought of him inside me.

I held his eyes as I popped the condom in my mouth before I sunk down on him. When I came back up, the condom was in place and it looked like the last of his self-control was gone.

He grabbed me by my hips and tossed me further up the bed, so my head landed on the pillows, before crawling over my body.

"Hang on tight, darlin'." Another command, but there was softness in his face.

He traced my opening and then sunk inside me in one smooth thrust.

My eyes closed at the perfect fit of him. My legs locked around his waist, my hands clasped behind his neck. He blew out a long breath into my neck.

"Addy," he groaned.

"Bell," I sighed.

"You feel so amazing."

I smiled as our lips met, and I opened my eyes to see him gazing at me with wonder.

"You need to move," I panted.

"Anything for you, my love."

He started slowly, giving me just enough to drive me crazy. Our breaths mixed as we stared at each other.

I'd never had sex like this before. I felt our connection humming through my veins, sparking along my synapses as he thrust into me, and I knew from the look in his eyes that he felt it too. He was right there with me.

I clenched around him and he dropped his head with a groan.

"Do that again," he commanded.

So I did. With every thrust I clenched around him, and soon the languid pace he'd had was a piston.

I held on for dear life as our souls climbed higher and higher. I caught Bell's lips with mine and then pulled back as I came right to the edge.

"I love you," I said as I shattered around him.

He followed right after me, chanting "I love you" over and over in my ear.

As our breathing evened out, he stayed inside me, working me through the aftershocks, before slowly pulling out.

He kissed my forehead as he got up and went into the bathroom. He came back with a warm towel and ran it over my entire body, his touch almost holy. Then he cleaned himself, tossed the towel into the bathroom, and settled against the headboard. He pulled me into him and wrapped his arms around me.

"I love you so much, Addy," he whispered.

I rested my head against his chest and listened to his heartbeat.

"I love you more than I ever thought I could love anyone," I admitted.

I felt his smile as he ran his fingers through my hair. Then he pulled the blankets over us, and I fell asleep to the steady sound of his heart in my ear.

Chapter Sixteen

Addy

Things with Bell were at a whole new level. He was slowly moving his things into my apartment.

We'd had an entire conversation about it in bed one morning. He knew I'd be hesitant, but after our confessions to each other I also knew that I needed to be with him as much as I could. I never wanted to be away from him. He'd told me that we could wait, that he was more than willing to commute between our places, and that just made me want to live with him more. We'd decided on mine because he knew I was more comfortable there, and he said he didn't mind either way. He wanted me to feel safe and in control. I loved him so much.

He'd met my parents. We'd invited them over for dinner so they could finally meet him. My mom just about swooned, and my dad even looked a little lost at first. They both adored him, and my mom had pulled me aside to tell me that she could tell he was head over heels in love with me.

He hadn't missed the significance of the introduction. My dad didn't know everything that happened with Derek, but he knew enough. Mom knew everything. They were insanely protective of me, especially after the attack, and they put Bell through the ringer.

He answered all of their questions with no hesitation and complete honesty, and that's what won them over, I think.

We'd gone on an official double date with Raelynn and Johnny, inviting them out to The Bell Tower.

They were both impressed that he owned it, and he and Johnny spent the whole night going through the brewing process and bitching about city ordinances on construction. Johnny was an architect, and he had actually been a big part in the city's renovation plans for the warehouse that had become The Bell Tower.

It was amazing, watching Bell interact with my friends. He was engaging and charming and would totally focus on the person he was conversing with. But his body never turned away from mine. He made sure he was always nearby, just in case I needed or wanted him. He checked in with me frequently.

He also couldn't keep his damn hands off me. Which, I couldn't lie, I loved. Whether he was linking our fingers together, or rubbing soft circles on my thigh with his thumb, or hooking his arm around me to pull me closer to him, there was always some point of contact between us.

It made me feel safe and cherished and so, so loved. No matter what else was going on around us, Bell was always letting me know that he was there.

He was like that at home too. Always just a call away, always respectful of my space. I hadn't realized that everybody I'd dated before Bell hadn't been a man.

They'd been boys, needing to be looked after and cared for. Bell looked after and cared for *me*. He cooked dinner, planned dates, and did laundry. I didn't let him take sole responsibility for all of that, we split it fairly evenly, but if he knew I'd had a hard day, he would be waiting for me with a glass of wine and snacks when I got home, ready to hear all about it. We usually never made it to the snacks.

That was the other thing about living with Bell. I got to experience the raw sexual chemistry that had sparked to life that night in the bar when he'd leaned in and whispered, *"I was thinking about how good you'd look spread out on my bed."*

He was dominating and bossy but took such good care of me. It was more than intense, and every day my love for him grew deeper and deeper. And I knew that he felt the same. It was like our souls were meant to exist in harmony with each other.

We were lying in bed one night after making love, and his fingers were playing with the hair at the nape of my neck.

"What are you thinking about?" I asked, because even after all this time his thoughts were still hidden from me. He could always read every thought on my face, but his was inscrutable.

He hummed for a moment, and I knew he was trying to find the words to articulate his thoughts. Finally, he said, "I was just thinking about fate. Do you believe in fate, Addy?"

"I didn't, before I met you," I confessed.

"I was just thinking the same thing," he laughed softly. "Everything before you in my life was leading me to this moment, and now looking back I wouldn't change a single thing. Everything led to the love of my life, and if that isn't fate then I don't know what to call it."

I pushed myself up on my elbow so I could trace his jaw with my fingertips.

"I just like to call it love," I smiled.

His eyes melted and he kissed me softly.

I smiled and settled back against his chest, feeling sleep coming. I had never been happier.

***

"I've got a few meetings today, so I might be home late," I said to Bell as I waited for the crossing light to turn. "Do you want me to pick anything up for dinner?"

"Chinese sounds good," he said. I could tell he was distracted, and I smiled to myself. It was payroll day.

"Chinese it is."

The light changed and as I stepped out into the street a car came whipping around the corner. I jumped back onto the sidewalk as my heart pounded in my chest. The car slowed slightly, and I thought they might get out to apologize, so I turned to wait for them when a chill ran down my spine.

It was the same blue Camaro I'd seen outside of my work a few times. The windows were tinted, so I couldn't see the driver, but I recognized the dent in the left fender and the Bigfoot sticker on the back window.

Was this car following me? Had it deliberately tried to run me down?

I took a step toward it, my hand shaking, and it raced off.

"Addy, are you alright?" Bell's voice sounded distant, and I realized I'd let my hand holding my phone drop to my side.

I quickly brought it back to my ear. "I'm okay, Bell, sorry. Some jackass ran the light, but I'm fine."

"Thank god, I heard the tires and was worried when you weren't responding," his voice had an edge of panic to it.

I blinked in the direction the car had gone, my mind trying to follow it. "Yeah, sorry. I'm fine though, really. I'll pick up Chinese on my way home tonight."

"Okay," he sounded hesitant to hang up.

His pause snapped me back into the moment. I let out the breath I'd been holding and smiled into the phone.

"You have payroll to do, mister, so I will see you when I get home."

"You're right, as usual," he sighed.

"I love you," I said softly.

"I love you more."

I grinned. "I love you most."

"Not possible."

This had become the way we said goodbye, and I always let him believe that he'd won.

"Bye, Bell."

"Goodbye, gorgeous."

***

I stumbled through the front door weighed down with way too much Chinese food. Bell immediately jumped up from the couch and took some of the bags, lightening my load. I smiled and kissed his cheek.

"How was your day?" I said in a sing-song voice as we got out plates and utensils.

"You know how much I loathe payroll," he said with an eye roll. "But I got through it and look at my reward."

He stepped back to gesture to me and I gave a small curtsy. His eyes danced and he took my hand and twirled me into his chest.

"Have I told you today how beautiful you are?" he whispered into my hair as we swayed in the kitchen.

"Mmmm, not since lunch, I don't think," I giggled.

He twirled me around and dipped me backwards, his lips kissing up my chest. When he got to my lips, he nipped them gently and pulled me upright.

"You're absolutely gorgeous, and I'm seriously considering

eating you for dinner instead," he said roughly in my ear.

Adrenaline shot through me. Bell didn't say things like that unless he meant to follow through with it.

I bit my lip, wondering if I should push it. I was starving but having Bell naked and underneath me sounded much better at the moment.

"We have a microwave," was all I said.

It was letting him know I was okay to skip eating, while still allowing him to do the seducing, which was my favorite thing he did. Bell was a master of seduction.

I'd never been someone who needed much foreplay, but it was Bell's favorite part of sex. He'd spend the better part of an hour warming me up, bringing me to the edge again and again, and I could tell he was enjoying it maybe even more than I was.

I watched his eyes flash in that way they did before he scooped me up and carried me into the bedroom.

Chinese food was better cold anyway.

***

I was sitting on the couch with my bowl of oatmeal the next morning when Bell came into the room fresh from the shower.

His towel was wrapped around his waist, his chest still wet, and my heart immediately started pounding in my chest.

I licked my lips as I looked him up and down, and it was only when my eyes settled on his lips that I realized he'd been speaking to me. I blinked a few times and the heat rushing to my face must have tipped him off as to where my thoughts had wandered.

"Jesus, Addy, you sex maniac," he teased, folding his arms, and leaning against the doorway. "Could you focus for two seconds without objectifying me?"

"Well, you look so damn delicious I couldn't help it," I smirked.

He laughed. "As I was saying, what would you say to taking a long weekend this week for a surprise?"

My eyes narrowed. "What kind of surprise?"

"The normal kind of surprise where you don't know what it is." He rolled his eyes.

I stuck my tongue out at him and watched his face change. He started walking very slowly towards the couch, his gaze laser focused on me. My eyes widened as I realized the game we were suddenly playing. One of my favorites.

I set my bowl down and slowly backed off the couch, keeping the distance between us. His tongue flashed across his bottom lip as he moved more deliberately toward me.

The corners of my mouth twisted up before I could stop them, and his eyes flashed. He darted toward me and I managed to get around the couch and past him into the hallway. I heard his feet squeak on the hardwood floors as he turned to chase me.

A giggle escaped as I slowed just enough for him to almost catch up, and then I took off again toward the bedroom. I reached the doorway when I felt his strong arms wrap around my waist and lift me into the air. My laughter echoed off the windows as he spun me around and tossed me on the bed, climbing over me and pinning my arms above my head with his hands.

Our eyes locked as our chests heaved from our chase, and electricity buzzed between us.

He leaned in and placed his lips against mine, not kissing, just holding them there.

"Yes or no to your surprise, Adelaide?"

A shiver ran down me when he said my name.

"Yes," I breathed. "You know I'll always say yes to you."

I felt his smile against my lips.

"Good."

Needless to say, we were both late to work that day.

Chapter Seventeen

Addy

I'd taken Friday and Monday off, so I'd been putting in extra hours at work to make up for it. I was exhausted, but it was finally Thursday. I'd made it. I was wrapping up the last details on a project before I headed off to my surprise weekend with Bell.

He was picking me up from work and we were heading straight to our destination, which was still a mystery to me.

My feet were tapping with excitement as it got closer and closer to quitting time.

Bell had been very strict all week with not telling me what the surprise was. Every tactic I'd tried had been either shot down or punished in the most delicious way possible.

I was usually uncomfortable not knowing what the plans were going to be, but I wasn't that way with Bell. And I knew that he really *knew* me and wouldn't plan something that wouldn't be enjoyable for me. It was stepping out of my comfort zone and trusting him, and it was a pretty big step for me, but it was such an exciting one.

Finally, the time on my computer said six o'clock, and I clocked out and grabbed my things in a hurry. I smiled when I saw Bell's silhouette against the frosted glass of the front door to the office.

I opened the door and bounced over to him, excitement coming off me in waves.

"Are you going to tell me where we're going yet?"

His face split into a slow smile and he took my jaw in his hand and kissed me softly. "Not yet, darlin', but you'll figure it out soon enough."

"Bell," I whined, stepping into his arms and playing with the collar of his shirt. "Please? A hint?"

"Nope," he smirked.

I tilted my head down and looked up at him. I placed a soft kiss right above the line of his shirt on the exposed skin of his neck.

"Please?"

I heard his sharp intake of breath, but he said nothing.

I placed another kiss right under his ear.

"Please?"

His breathing stuttered, and I thought I had him, but then he shook his head.

My eyes narrowed and I brought his face down to mine and kissed him deeply. Our tongues swept together and in that moment it was just us. I forgot what I'd been trying to do as I was swept up in the heat of his body on mine. When we pulled away, his eyes were out of focus as he stared at me.

That's right. Answers. I was trying to get answers.

"Please?" I arched an eyebrow.

He looked at me for a long time before producing a set of keys that had previously been in my jacket pocket. I hadn't even felt him take them. He turned and locked the office door behind me.

I pouted a moment and felt something twinge in my chest. Some deeper feeling rose in my throat, and I was suddenly blinking back tears. He noticed, and his fingers came to my chin.

"What's going on, Addy?"

I looked at him as I tried to place the strange feeling I was having. Insecurity, it suddenly dawned on me.

"Are you really so unaffected by me?" I asked, nodding at the keys in his hands.

He looked confused, and then his eyes cleared and confusion was replaced with soft sweetness.

"Addy, you're the most enchanting creature God ever created. You're a constant distraction, and I have never and will never come close to being unaffected by you," he said gently. His eyes flashed and he pulled me close to him, and I could feel his erection against my stomach. "That's how affected I am by you, missy."

I felt a smile creep onto my face, and he kissed my cheek.

"I love you, Adelaide Jones, and if I have to prove it to you every day of our lives I will gladly do so."

"But you won't tell me where we're going?"

He blinked at me and then laughed loud and deep. He dropped a kiss onto my forehead. "Nope."

I sighed in defeat and shrugged my shoulders. "Fine, I concede. Lead the way, mister."

He took my arm in his and led me to the street.

"Hey, that's a nice car," he suddenly remarked. "With a little bit of restoration work, it could be worth a bit of money."

My brow furrowed and I followed his gaze across the street.

My heart stuttered.

Dent in the fender. Bigfoot sticker. Tinted windows.

It was the same Camaro I'd been seeing for weeks. The same Camaro that had almost hit me last week, and then had taken off.

Something about that car made my blood run cold. Was it following me? Who was the driver? Was I in danger? Should I tell Bell?

Then the rational part of my brain kicked in.

'Don't be silly.' I told myself. *'They probably work on the street. They're not following you. And the other day they were probably just late or something and didn't see you crossing. There's nothing suspicious going on, Addy. You're being paranoid. Besides, you don't want to tell Bell because he'll get all protective, and that will ruin the trip. It's nothing to worry about.'*

I took a deep breath as we continued walking, vowing to put that stupid old Camaro out of my head once and for all.

***

We pulled up to the airport and my excitement continued to grow. We were flying somewhere?

Bell magically produced two bags from the back of the car and threw me a wink.

"You packed for me?"

"I'd hardly call it packing, you only own twelve outfits, Addy," he smirked. "In fact, I had to do a bit of shopping for this trip."

"You didn't." My horrified face reflected in the car window.

His grin widened. "Oh, but I did."

"*Where* are you taking me?" I pleaded once more, but my heart wasn't really in it. Bell had been doing such a good job keeping it a secret that I didn't want him to ruin it before he had to.

He tutted and kissed my temple. "All in good time, darlin'."

I rolled my eyes and took my bag from him. I was tempted to look through it, but he grabbed my hand and pulled me along toward the terminal.

We made our way to the check in line, and he turned to me and kissed me gently.

"Where's the one place you've always wanted to go, but never had the time?" he asked me, intertwining our fingers.

My eyes narrowed as I thought. I'd never been anywhere, and I wasn't much for travel. Raelynn was the travel bug, always jetting off to foreign lands and adventures. I preferred the predictability of staying at home.

But there was one place that I'd been dreaming about visiting since I was a child. I'd never had the money to do it properly, so I'd never gone.

"New York City?" I gasped, my heart fluttering.

A huge grin spread across his face, and that was all the confirmation I needed.

I dropped my bag and threw myself into his arms. He caught me with one arm and spun me around before dropping me to the ground and leaning his head against mine.

"And here I was worried you wouldn't want to go," he teased.

I playfully smacked his chest before bending to pick up my bag. I was flying to New York City for the weekend with my demigod boyfriend. I had never been happier.

***

"Bell," I breathed as we entered the hotel suite he'd booked.

The far wall was glass, showing a beautiful view of the city. Tall ceilings and white walls made the space feel enormous, and it was furnished with muted leather furniture and recycled wood accents. I floated through the living space and found myself in the bedroom, where my jaw dropped.

A luxurious king size bed was placed in the center of the room and fitted with the softest looking bedding I'd seen in my life. Sheer white curtains hung from the four-poster bed frame, swaying softly in the breeze from the air conditioner. I'd never felt the urge to run and leap onto a bed, but damned if that wasn't the first thing on my mind. My bag dropped out of my stunned fingers as I took the room in.

I felt Bell's hands creep around my waist and pull me back against him.

"Do you like it?"

"Bell, it's perfect," I sighed. "You're perfect."

"I'd have to be to deserve you," he kissed the nape of my neck gently.

I melted into his arms as he peppered kisses down my shoulder and then back up my jaw. I looked up at him from over my shoulder and saw his eyes shining. Then, that familiar glint came into them and I was suddenly lifted, spun, and thrown onto the bed. I giggled as I bounced and Bell stood at the end of the bed, watching me.

"The plans I have for you, Adelaide Jones," he purred.

My stomach fluttered and I felt myself start to tingle. I got up onto my hands and knees and crawled over to him. Taking his shirt in my hands, I pulled him down roughly for a kiss.

We made out for what seemed like forever, and his hands had drifted to my ass, kneading and pulling me into him. I ground my hips against his growing erection as we panted into each other's mouths. My fingers dropped to undo the button on his pants, and suddenly his hands had mine in a vice grip. I looked up at him, confusion on my face, and saw something raw and carnal flash through his eyes.

"We have somewhere to be in an hour," he whispered, bringing my wrist up to his lips and kissing it tenderly.

"So, you're just going to get me all riled up and then not deliver?" I whined, thrusting my hips forward so that I could tease him.

"You started it," he muttered, his eyes closing at the contact. He still hadn't released my wrists, and my core was throbbing.

"Please, Bell," I panted. "I need you."

His eyes opened and flashed wickedly. That devilish grin lit up his face, and he pushed me backwards and straddled my hips, lifting my hands over my head and pinning them there. I loved when he dominated me like this, taking over my body like it was his plaything.

Our eyes locked, and he kissed the middle of my chest. He licked his way up to my ear, where he whispered, "I'll be in the shower. Check the closet for your first surprise."

Then, he was gone. I heard the lock on the bathroom door click, and I smirked to myself. He knew I would have just followed him in. Smart man.

I let my body relax into the bed as I tried to calm the throbbing between my legs. What a way to begin a trip.

After I'd calmed down, I went to the closet and slowly opened the door. Inside was a gorgeous cocktail dress made of deep red silk. It looked to be an off the shoulder, knee length dress. The skirt was beautifully ruffled with chiffon layers underneath the draping fabric. I sighed and my hand flew over my heart.

No one had ever bought me anything like it before. It was stunning. There were a pair of strappy black heels underneath it that would go with any number of outfits, and a black shawl draped on another hanger next to the dress.

I heard the shower turn off and felt Bell's presence when he walked back in the room. I was so aware of him, and I couldn't help the physical response I had to him. My heart stuttered, my breath caught, and all I wanted to do was run into his arms.

I turned to thank him, and my brain malfunctioned. The towel wrapped around his waist was almost too small, as most hotel towels tend to be, and it showed off his muscular thighs and toned stomach.

And the smell wafting off of him had me nearly delirious. I blinked as I tried to regain some semblance of thought.

"The dress is gorgeous," I finally managed.

"It'll look better with you in it," he winked.

I laughed and ran a hand through my hair.

"Well, if you expect me to be ready to go in less than an hour, then I need the bathroom and total privacy," I said, rushing past him.

He caught my arm and spun me back so that he could quickly kiss me before releasing me to go get ready.

***

There's something about New York City at night that leaves you breathless, but it was nothing compared to seeing Bell in a perfectly tailored suit. I hadn't been able to appreciate the visual as much as I'd wanted, because as soon as I was ready he'd swept me out of the hotel and into a whirlwind night.

We'd been to a five-star restaurant, had our food brought to us by the chef personally (apparently, he was an old friend of Bell's from his college days), danced to live jazz music in Central Park, and were currently making our way back to the hotel.

Cars meandered past us, fighting through traffic even this late at night. But instead of being annoyed by it, I was amazed by the glow of the taillights on Bell's face.

I was floating. I clung to Bell's arm as the magic of the night washed over me yet again.

"Can I ask you something?"

"You can ask me anything, anytime, anywhere, darlin'."

"I don't want to sound like I'm complaining, but…" I chewed my lip. This had been niggling at the back of my brain since we'd landed, but I wasn't sure how to phrase it.

"C'mon Addy," Bell coaxed, bumping me with his shoulder. "Just spit it out."

"Okay," I sighed. "How did you afford this trip? I know the restaurant is doing well, but you've got loans to pay back and all of the overhead costs. I hate to think of you spending money you don't necessarily have on…me."

Bell pulled me into an alcove just off the sidewalk and took my face in his hands.

"You and that worrisome brain of yours," he said softly, his eyes warm as he searched my face.

"I love that you're worried for me. That you don't need me to spoil you," he said. "That being said, you'd better get used to being spoiled."

"That didn't answer my question," I pointed out.

He laughed and it took the edge off of the chill in the air.

"I made a few very good investment choices right after college," he explained. "I've continued to make good investments since. I'm not exactly strapped for cash, Addy."

"Oh."

"Not that I wouldn't put myself in an immovable amount of debt for you." He gave me a quick kiss and then hooked my arm through his and navigated us back to the stream of people on the sidewalk.

"I didn't grow up with a lot. Pops did everything he could, and we were comfortable, but he taught me the value of making my money work for me very young. I just happened to make a couple of good choices after school, and it set me up to continue making good choices. I also have worked every day since I graduated, and have saved a lot of that money too."

I thought about the decent size of my savings account and couldn't help the laugh that bubbled out of me.

"What?" he asked.

"You're just full of surprises, that's all," I said happily. "You'll have to teach me how to invest someday soon. I can't let you be the only one paying for surprises."

He laughed and squeezed my arm lovingly. "It's a deal. The second we get back, Economics 101 will begin."

We walked in silence for awhile, weaving in and out of other pedestrians. I loved how alive I felt in that city, with that man.

I could never have imagined Addy from after the attack taking a chance on a surprise trip with her boyfriend. I couldn't have imagined her having a boyfriend. So much had changed since Bell had come into my life, and I was suddenly overwhelmed with how much I loved him.

"Bell, this was the perfect night," I sighed, leaning my head against his shoulder as we walked. The wine I'd had with dinner was still buzzing around my bloodstream, making the lights softer and the beating of my heart faster.

"Almost perfect," Bell said softly, dropping a kiss to the top of my head.

I looked at him challengingly. "Oh? Almost? And what would make this night perfect for you?"

He grinned and pulled me tightly against his body. He lowered his lips to my ear and his breath sent shivers down my back. He never broke his stride, and I had to pay attention to keep from stumbling over my feet.

"It will be perfect when I'm buried so deep inside of you that you can't tell where you end and I begin," he growled.

My breath caught in my throat and I felt heat drop to my core.

The rest of the walk back to the hotel was tense. I could feel every spot that our bodies touched. The heat from his skin seeped into my bones. His eyes kept meeting mine and fanning the spark

174

that he'd ignited.

Finally, *finally*, we made it back to the hotel.

He let me in before him, and the silence of the room washed over me. In the darkness, the city lights sparkled through the windows. I heard the click of the door locking, and my heart pounded in my chest. I marveled that he could still affect me the same way he'd done when we first met.

I kept my gaze on the city in front of me as I stood in front of the window. His fingers skimmed up my arms, leaving goosebumps in their wake. He found the zipper of my dress and slowly slid it down. The fabric rustled softly as it pooled on the floor.

Then, his strong hands wrapped around my shoulders and his lips brushed against the nape of my neck. My breath caught in my throat and my eyes closed. I was lost in the feel of his skin on mine.

My head fell back against his chest and he reached around to slip a hand into my panties.

"Do you think they can see you?" he whispered.

My head whipped up and I looked out of the window and saw people milling around on the street below.

"You'd better hope they can't," I said with a playful slap on his wrist.

He hummed softly and then slid a long finger inside of me. It took me by surprise, and my head immediately fell back against him again.

"Do you think I could make you not care?" he said, a challenge in his voice.

"I highly doubt it," I said, relishing the feel of his finger moving in and out of me.

I felt his smile against my neck as he bit my pulse point gently and added a second finger. His other hand moved around to circle the tingling bud of nerves that always betrayed me. He played with me for a moment, bringing me to gasping breaths, my fingers digging into his thighs. Just when I was about to fall, he pulled away and spun me around.

"Let me fuck you against the window?" he growled.

It wasn't a command, but a question. I knew he wouldn't do anything I wasn't comfortable with, but he'd done such a good job getting me going that I would have let him fuck me on the street just to feel him inside of me.

As an answer, I jumped into his arms and wrapped my legs around his waist. As he steadied me, I reached down and undid his pants, pushing his clothes down just enough to release his weeping cock. I stroked it a few times and he backed me up against the window.

I held his eyes as I shoved my panties to the side and positioned him at my entrance.

He looked at me questioningly. We'd never gone bare before, but I'd had us both get tested a few weeks ago.

"We're both clean, and I'm on the pill," I whispered, holding his gaze as I rubbed him along my lips. "I want to feel all of you."

He bit back a groan when I squeezed him and lowered myself onto the tip. He thrust up into me, sheathing himself. Our moans mingled in the air, and I wrapped my arms around his neck. He braced his hands on the window and then took me for all of New York City to see.

Chapter Eighteen

Addy

The rest of the weekend was just as magical as that first night. We saw Broadway shows, ate at expensive restaurants, did all of the touristy things we could, and spent every night tangled in those luxurious sheets. And then, just as quickly as it had started, it was over and we were packing our bags to fly home.

On the flight home I was consumed with thoughts about how *right* it felt to be with Bell. He made me feel safe and loved and protected, but he never tried to control me. He let me live my own life, and he never got overly jealous or possessive.

Physically we were beyond compatible. My body responded to him without my conscious permission. It wanted to submit to his every desire, and he always prioritized me and my contentment. I smiled whenever I thought about him, so I was always smiling.

Whenever a trigger from my past came up, he was supportive but not overbearing. He gave me space, but was always there when I needed him to be. We had such open and honest communication between us that we were in tune with each other in a way I'd never experienced.

I was in love with him. I wanted to spend the rest of my life with him. It was terrifying to admit, even in my head, but I couldn't hide from the truth of it. I couldn't imagine a life without him in it now. I never wanted to be without Bell.

***

I was early to work, wanting to catch up after my long weekend. As I crossed the street to my office, I was fumbling to find the right key, so I didn't notice the figure in the doorway at first.

By the time I looked up it was too late to turn around. My heart stopped.

"Who the fuck was that guy?" Derek's angry voice came from the shadow of the overhang.

Panic flooded my veins, and my mind threatened to send me back two years, but I couldn't let it. Derek was here. Now. And I had to deal with that.

I swallowed around the rock in my throat and steeled myself.

"You need to leave," I managed to spit out from between clenched teeth.

"Some guy picks you up and then you don't show up to work for two days," he ranted. "Who the fuck is he, Ads?"

He stepped out of the shadow and I saw that he wasn't right. He wasn't the dewy eyed, tan-skinned heartthrob from my memories. His skin was sallow, his eyes hollow and haunted. He'd lost weight and his clothes hung from him.

I took a step back as he approached and looked around, hoping someone would be coming. But it was still early, and I was alone. Alone with a man who was clearly in the middle of a psychotic break.

"It's none of your business," I hissed, adrenaline pumping through me.

"The fuck it isn't!"

I flinched and the sound of glass breaking echoed in my head. I gripped my bag tightly and kept moving away from him.

He saw me react and his face dropped. But the sadness didn't reach his eyes. It looked forced. He stopped walking towards me, and a bit of relief rippled through me as I realized I might still be able to get away from him.

"Ads, I'm sorry baby, you know I wouldn't hurt you. Please, don't be scared of me. I just...I need to talk to you."

My eyes widened in disbelief. "I don't want anything to do with you. Go away."

He sighed and held his hands up in surrender. "Okay, I get it. I'm sorry, I just got crazy jealous when I saw him with you."

I glared at him and didn't move. There was nothing I could say to that. What world of delusion was he living in where he had any right to be jealous of the people in my life? Bile rose in my throat, but I forced myself to hold his gaze.

"I'll go," he muttered, backing away from the doorway.

I watched him for a moment and did the risk assessment in my head. He moved further away, and I was overwhelmed with the need to be inside the office with the door locked.

I moved to the doorway quickly, watching him the entire time. When he realized I didn't trust him, he sighed sadly and walked away.

I followed him with my eyes for a moment, and then began frantically flipping through the keys to find the right one. I finally found it and unlocked the door. I got the door open, and then a hand was wrapped around my forearm.

Derek ripped me away from the door and flung me onto the sidewalk. Sharp pain laced through me as instinct took over and I landed directly on my ass. At least I didn't try to break the fall with my hands and end up snapping a wrist. The contact with the ground sent a numbing pain up my spine and I collapsed onto my side.

"You think you can do better than me?" he shouted.

His foot connected with my stomach and the air left my lungs.

I blinked through the pain, using it to focus my mind. I wasn't the same woman he'd attacked before. I was stronger. Smarter. Braver.

When he swung his leg again, I rolled into him, knocking him onto the ground as I struggled to get up.

He was faster than I was and was on his feet in an instant.

My brain was working overtime as my fight or flight instincts kicked in.

He threw his arm out and I stepped around him and connected my elbow with his stomach.

He doubled over, but still managed to shove me out into the street.

My feet stumbled over the curb and I caught my fall with my hands and knees. I felt blood trickling down my shins as I slipped my ballet flats off. I was going to run.

And then he was on top of me.

His body pinned me to the ground, his hand grinding my face into the asphalt.

I managed to flip myself over, but as I did so his fist smashed into my nose.

My vision blurred and colors bloomed behind my eyes.

I growled through the blood that filled my mouth and threw my elbow at his face.

There was a satisfying crunch as bone connected with bone, and I heard his shout as he fell off of me.

I stood quickly, adrenaline keeping the pain at bay, and kicked with all of the hatred and fear that had been building inside of me.

He curled onto his side, blood streaming from the cracked skin on his cheek.

My leg cocked back to kick him again, but I couldn't do it.

"I'm not like you," I spat at him, realizing that I couldn't attack him just because I wanted to hurt him. I wasn't that person.

I took a few steps away from him. I didn't hear the car horn as a driver raced around the corner.

***

Pain was the first thing I registered. My eyes weren't open, but when I scrunched my nose, pain bloomed from the center of my face.

Then it was in my abdomen. My left wrist.

I tried desperately to think of why I would be hurting so badly.

It came to me in flashes.

Derek standing in the shadows.

The smell of the asphalt in my nose as my face connected with the ground.

The honk of a car horn.

The crunch of glass.

Then…nothing.

If I wasn't so tired, I might've heard Bell's voice comforting my mom and dad, or the beeping of monitors. But instead sleep took me away again.

***

"Good morning, gorgeous," Bell's soft voice greeted me when I finally opened my eyes.

I blinked a few times and winced when it hurt.

"Even I know I'm not gorgeous right now," I croaked.

Bell smiled, though his eyes were sad, and lifted a cup with a straw to my mouth.

"Drink," he ordered.

As always, my body obeyed his commands. The water felt like new life as it went through my body.

"So, what's the damage?" I sighed.

Bell sat gingerly on the hospital bed, his hand resting on my arm.

"Broken nose, they reset it so it shouldn't look too different," he said soberly. "You sprained your wrist when you fell. There was no internal bleeding in your stomach, but you've got some nasty bruises. Luckily, the car didn't do much damage past some road rash and cuts from the windshield. Doc said you were really lucky. It could've been a lot worse."

Our eyes met, and I was suddenly overwhelmed. Tears pricked at the corner of my eyes.

"I was so scared, Bell," I whispered. My body began to shake as it started to process the shock of what had happened.

Bell leaned down and rested his head on my chest, being careful not to jostle any of my injuries. I knew it must be killing him not to be able to just hold me. And that was all I wanted from him.

I pushed myself up as best as I could, wincing through the pain and the tears, until he managed to catch me, his arm wrapping behind my back to support me.

In his arms, I cried.

I cried because I was in pain. I cried because I was angry. I cried because I was scared.

And I cried because the last time I was in the hospital because of Derek I couldn't even let the male doctor examine me, and now I had Bell holding me, making me feel safe and protected.

He muttered sweet comforts into my hair and rubbed my back as my panic eventually subsided.

I looked up at him through bleary eyes and offered a weak smile.

"God, Addy," he breathed. "You're so strong. I'm constantly amazed by you."

"I love you so much," I whispered.

He smiled and gently pressed his lips to mine. I winced a little at the pressure but didn't move away.

When he pulled back his eyes were cloudy.

"Um," he cleared his throat. "Your parents are here, and so is Raelynn."

I sighed. "I'll talk to them in a bit. Right now I just want to be here with you."

"One more thing," he hesitated. I looked expectantly at him, and he ran a finger down the side of my neck. "The police are here. There's CCTV footage of the attack, and they were able to identify Derek, so they want to talk to you and get your statement."

I took a deep breath and nodded once. He looked at me for a long moment before slowly leaving the room.

When he returned, he had two police officers in tow, a young man and an older woman. The woman had clearly briefed the younger officer to let her take the lead, and he stood by the door while she approached the bedside with a soft smile.

"Ms. Jones, I'm Detective Herald. How are you feeling?"

"Like I was hit by a car."

She chuckled softly. Her eyes were warm, and the small smile on her lips had me trusting her instantly.

"We watched the CCTV footage, so we know the basics of what happened," she started. She took out a notebook and flicked through some pages before her gaze returned to me. "We were able to identify your attacker as Derek Johnson, who has multiple warrants out for his arrest. Unfortunately, he'd fled the scene by the time the ambulance and police arrived, but we were able to follow him on the cameras to his car."

"Is it an old Camaro?" My voice was barely a whisper.

Surprise flitted across the face of everyone in the room.

"Yes," the woman said gently. "How did you know that?"

I took a breath, my eyes flitting to Bell before coming back to hers. "I'd noticed an old blue Camaro following me around the last few weeks. I thought it might just be someone who worked on the street, so I didn't want to worry anyone about it."

Bell's eyes iced over and I saw the muscle in his jaw clench, but he said nothing. Surely, he was remembering how he'd complimented the car just a few days ago.

"I see," the policewoman said, making a note in her pad.

"What are his warrants for?" I asked, twisting the rough hospital blanket in my fingers.

She looked at me for a moment, and then countered with, "Can you tell me why he attacked you?"

My eyes narrowed, but I knew they'd need to know that eventually.

"Bell picked me up from work last week. We went to New York for a long weekend. I guess Derek was watching us, and he got jealous. I haven't spoken to him in almost two years, but for some reason he was upset that I was seeing someone. He was furious. I told him to go away, and he looked like he was leaving, so I rushed to get into the office, but it took me a minute to find the right key. I was panicking, so I didn't hear him come back."

The detective nodded, writing down my statement. Then, she let out a heavy breath.

"In the two years since Derek last put you in the hospital, he's

184

beaten and raped multiple women in the surrounding counties, always managing to escape before police arrive."

I felt bile rising in my throat, thinking about the women that he'd been hurting. Was it because of me? Because I'd cut him out of my life?

"He's also heavily involved in drug running for a local gang," the detective continued.

That explained why he looked so sick. Drugs.

"How are you going to catch him?" I asked, my voice rising an octave in distress. "He can't keep hurting people, so how are you going to bring him in?"

She was silent for a moment before settling gently on the edge of the hospital bed.

"That's another thing I wanted to talk to you about," she said softly. "We know now that Derek clearly, in his own deranged and twisted way, still cares for you. We think you might be the only one he would be open to meeting."

"Meeting?" Bell interjected. "As in, in person? After what he just did to her? Are you insane?" His voice was low, defensive.

"Would it get him locked up? Off the street?" I asked, ignoring Bell.

"Yes. We have testimony and DNA evidence that prove he committed the crimes, we just haven't been able to catch him."

Silence settled over the room, and I finally forced myself to look at Bell.

His face was a study in disbelief. He looked lost, angry, confused, worried. Detective Harold followed my gaze and then patted my hand.

"I'll let you think about it for a bit, but with your help Adelaide... we could bring him to justice. For good."

She stood and put her business card on the bedside table.

"Call me when you've made a decision. The longer we wait, the more chance there is he hurts someone else."

Then they were gone, the door clicking shut behind them. And it was just me and Bell. I watched him for a moment, waiting for him to say something, but I could tell his mind was going a thousand miles a minute. His gaze was locked on a corner of the room, glazed over.

"Bell." My voice broke him out of his trance and he stared at me.

"It's ridiculous, Addy," he growled, clearly continuing the stream-of-consciousness that had been running through his head. "They can't just use you like a puppet, putting you in harm's way. They should be doing their job without having to endanger your life."

"Bell –"

"How dare they ask you to do their fucking job for them? That maniac beats and rapes women, and they want you to volunteer to meet him? They want you to trust that they'll get there in time, when they so clearly haven't at any point in the past? It's unfair and absolutely not going to happen."

"Bell." My voice was sharp. His mouth snapped closed and his eyes looked at me, haunted.

"You can't be even considering this, Addy," he whispered.

I held out my hand and he intertwined our fingers gently, sitting on the bed with me.

"Look at what he did to you," he muttered, his other hand tracing the bruises on my skin. "I can't lose you, Addy."

"But what if he hurts someone else, and I could have stopped him?"

The question had been circling in my head since the detective told me what Derek's charges were. She had been right. He was clearly still attached to me for God knows what reason. If he had been hurting women these past few years because he couldn't get to me, then the only thing that I could do to make that up to the world was to get him arrested.

"It's not your responsibility, Adelaide!" Bell snapped.

I soothed my hand down his arm. "I know it's not. But I can't help feeling like I have to help."

"Addy, you ended up in the hospital because of him. Twice," Bell's voice was pleading, but I could tell he knew he couldn't talk me out of it.

"And what if the next time he attacks some poor woman she ends up dead?"

He had no response to that.

We sat there, hands clasped, for a long moment.

"I have to help catch him, Bell," I said softly. "They're right, I'm the only one that he would let his guard down enough to see in person. I'm the only one that can get him out of the world."

Bell watched me for a long time, his dark eyes unreadable. I couldn't imagine what he must be thinking. He was my protector, the love of my life, and I was talking about voluntarily confronting a man who had hurt me in every way imaginable.

I fully expected him to argue with me, so I was surprised when he closed his eyes and let out a deep sigh.

"I'm coming to every planning meeting, I'll know all of the details of the meetup, and I'll be right outside when you do meet him," he finally conceded, opening his eyes and finding mine so that I could see how serious he was. "No arguments."

I tried to smile but winced when pain lashed through my head.

His gaze softened, and he kissed the back of my hand.

"I can't lose you, Addy. It would break me," he confessed.

"You'll never lose me, Bell. I'm way too stubborn to let that happen," I joked.

He didn't laugh.

I sighed. I knew that he still didn't like the choice I was making, but it felt so very out of my hands. It was the only way to make sure nobody else got hurt. To make up for some of the pain Derek had caused.

Logically, I knew it wasn't my fault. Laura and I had worked very hard on that until it was something that I just knew. A fundamental belief. But just because it wasn't my fault didn't mean I could stand by and do nothing while innocent women were hurt.

Bell didn't have to like this. He just had to be there for me. That's all I needed.

"Why don't you go get my parents and Raelynn," I suggested, trying to ease some of the tension that had knifed its way between us. "They'll want to know I'm awake."

He nodded once and looked at me with those unfathomable eyes. Then he stood and placed a gentle kiss on the crown of my head. He was still with me, as much as he might disagree with my choices. He wasn't going to abandon me to the wolves. Well, wolf.

As he left the room, my eyes drifted shut. I took three deep breaths and steeled myself in my decision. Derek Johnson wouldn't hurt anyone else. Not if I could help it.

Chapter Nineteen

Addy

After a week in the hospital the doctors cleared me to go home. I still had to be very gentle with myself, but I could bathe and use the toilet on my own. The bruises on my face were at their worst, deep blues and purples tinged with sickly greens. It hurt every time I blinked.

Bell was quiet in the car on the drive home. He said nothing as he helped me up the stairs and into the apartment. He settled me in bed and left without saying a word.

He hadn't been very communicative since I'd called Detective Herald to let her know that I would help her bring Derek to justice.

I knew that he disagreed with the solution, but to me it was the only thing that made sense. I had to place my trust somewhere, and even if I didn't trust the police department as an institution, I knew I could trust Detective Herald to keep me safe.

When I woke, a few hours after we got home, I heard Bell in the kitchen. I wandered out, my body throbbing with the effort of moving.

"What are you making?" I asked softly.

He jumped. He must have been in lost in his thoughts and hadn't heard me come in.

He looked at me for a long moment, and I swear I saw tears welling in his eyes before he turned back to the stove.

"My Pop's chicken noodle soup." His voice was soft, deep and lined with pain.

"For me?"

"Of course, for you, silly." He tried to smile over his shoulder, but it wasn't the soul warming grin that I'd come to need like air.

My heart ached, and I just wanted to be close to him. I made my way into the kitchen and lifted one of his arms so I could snuggle against his chest. He was stiff at first, and then sighed deeply and relaxed his body against me.

"Are we okay?" I whispered into the tension.

"Addy…"

"I know you don't agree with what I'm doing…but I have to, Bell. You know my reasons. We've been over them a million times already. I just…I hate this space between us."

"I'm right here, Addy," he whispered into my hair.

"But you're not. Not really." I felt my throat constrict around tears I couldn't cry.

Bell didn't say anything. With one arm he held me, and with the other he continued to stir the broth and vegetables. I pressed my ear to his chest, trying to take comfort in his heartbeat, but I couldn't hear it.

He offered nothing. No comfort, no calming words. But he didn't let go of me, and *that* I could hold on to. He was processing this in his own way, but he wasn't leaving me.

After a long moment, Bell took a deep breath.

"Why don't you go crawl back into bed, and I'll bring some soup in for you. And then we'll put that cream on your eye that the doctor recommended."

Silently, I nodded.

Our bed was plush and comfortable but did nothing to soothe the ache in my chest when Bell gently dabbed cream on my face, handed me a bowl of soup, and then left the room.

As I ate, I couldn't stop thinking about the faceless women that Derek had assaulted over the years. I knew it wasn't my fault. But in my heart, it felt like it was. Derek had stalked me and beaten me because he'd seen I had a new man in my life. He clearly was still attached, even if it was just because of the way the drugs had ruined his mind.

If I called him, he'd come. He'd meet me. I was sure of it.

And when he did, he'd be arrested. He'd get locked in a cage for the rest of his life, and he wouldn't be able to hurt anyone ever again.

Bell may not have liked it, but this was the only solution.

***

It took another two weeks for me to feel comfortable going out into the world. Mainly because that's how long the bruises took to fade enough to be covered with makeup.

In those two weeks, Bell stayed distant.

He was the most caring and attentive nurse, bringing me food, making sure I took my medication, helping me with my physical therapy. He was a constant presence.

But he didn't touch me unless he needed to. We didn't speak about anything other than my recovery. Tension flooded the air every time we were in the same room.

I kept expecting him to realize that I needed his support and kept hoping he'd accept that the meet up was going to happen. He never did.

He was putting up walls between us, maintaining a distance

from me no matter how many times I reached out to bridge it. Every day he seemed to pull further away from me, and every day my heart cracked a little deeper.

I didn't know how to talk to him about any of this. I didn't know how to make him see what this distance between us was doing to me.

Breaking my heart. I felt like such a burden to him.

My first appointment out of the house was to the doctor, so they could give me the all-clear to head back to work. That went flawlessly. The doctor said that I was healing much more quickly than he'd expected, and that I should make a full recovery as long as I kept doing what I was doing.

My first thought was to call Bell and tell him the good news. My phone was in my hand, finger hovering over his name, when a little voice in my head stopped me.

What if he breaks up with you now that you're better? What if he was only staying to take care of you because he felt sorry for you?

I shook my head, trying to dispel the thoughts, but the longer I stared at his name on the screen, the louder the doubts became.

What if the reason that I'd been feeling like such a burden was because I was one? Because he really was only staying because he felt like he had to. And now that I was on the mend there was nothing forcing him to stay with me.

Angrily, I shoved my phone into my purse and took a few deep breaths. I was exhausted. The trip to the doctor had wiped all of my energy, and I needed to be home where I could think. The cab ride home was short, but it still gave me enough time for my thoughts about Bell to spiral into a dark place.

Having Bell in my life was like having my own personal sun. He lit me up, warmed me from the inside out. He had never judged me for my past and spent every second of every day reminding me that I was worthy of being loved. He worshiped my body, lavished

192

me with attention. He was gentle, but rough when I needed him to be.

It was like my entire life I'd been painting a picture, my life story weaving in and out of the strokes. It was a complete picture by itself, but then Bell came along and I suddenly realized that there was more to the painting. Another scene, beautiful in its own right, but perfectly complementary to mine. His picture didn't complete mine…it just gave it perspective, and somehow managed to make it even more beautiful.

I couldn't imagine going through life without him. I was irrevocably in love with the man. And I knew that I'd break his heart by going through with my plan to help capture Derek. Especially if something did go wrong, for some reason.

I let out a heavy breath when I realized Bell wasn't home. I was grateful. I needed to think, and I couldn't do that with the heartbreaking tension that had been so heavy in the house lately.

I made a quick cup of tea and settled on the couch, my mind swirling with melancholy thoughts. I was trying to avoid thinking about it, because if I could do that then I wouldn't have to let the hurt in.

The last thing in the world I wanted was for Bell to be staying with me out of obligation. And I just couldn't shake the gnawing fear that he was. That since the hospital, he'd only stayed to help me recover.

He didn't need someone else in his life to just up and disappear, like his mom did. I wouldn't force him to stay. But I wasn't sure I could say goodbye. I didn't think I was that strong.

Guilt overwhelmed me, and soon I was sobbing into my tea. Just the thought of losing Bell made me hyperventilate.

But it was the right thing to do. Just like confronting Derek was the right thing to do.

I needed to offer Bell his freedom, even if it meant I'd fall apart.

***

The apartment was quiet when Bell finally came home. I heard the locks click, and then his footsteps in the foyer stutter to a halt.

He'd seen my bag.

"Addy?" His voice was soft, hurt.

He knew exactly what was happening, but I was sure he'd make me say it anyway.

"The doctor gave me the all-clear," I said from the couch. "I still need to be careful, but I'm good to resume my life."

His eyes lifted to mine, and they looked haunted already. "That's great, Addy."

His gaze dropped to the bag by the door and I saw his shoulders slump.

"Going somewhere?"

I closed my eyes and took a deep breath.

"I'm going to stay at my parents' for a bit."

"Why?" His tone told me he knew the answer.

"Because we need some space. I've been a burden to you for long enough, and I want you to have space to think about if you still want to be with me."

The words tasted like ash in my mouth.

I glanced at Bell and saw that his face had shut down. He was staring through me, as if trying to make sense of my words, and a brick wall slammed down behind his eyes. It was the same wall he'd been building stone by stone throughout my recovery.

I watched him for a long moment, waiting, praying for him to tell me that he loved me. That he would support me and be there for me through this, and that we'd be okay.

Instead, he just stared at the ground.

Somewhere, I heard my heart shattering into a million little pieces.

A car honked from the street.

"That's Raelynn. I asked her to wait outside while we talked," I said softly.

Moving from the couch, I gently put on my shoes and picked up my bag. Bell was still immobile.

"Thank you for taking such good care of me lately. I know it was a lot, and I appreciate you sticking around even though you didn't want to," I murmured, too scared to look at him.

I touched his wrist gently and then left him standing in the hallway. When the door clicked shut, he still hadn't blinked.

Chapter Twenty

Bell

Waking up without Addy next to me was equivalent to waking up with a knife in my stomach. A physical pain so deep that it took me a moment to catch my breath. It didn't help that her scent was everywhere. On the pillows, the blankets, in the shower. I couldn't escape from her. Fuck, I was living in her goddamn apartment.

I kept replaying what she'd said two days ago when she left.

"I want you to have space to think about if you still want to be with me."

Why would she even think that I'd want to leave? It made absolutely no sense to me. I'd been there through her entire recovery, helping her, nursing her back to health. I'd thought that I'd been showing her that I was with her, always.

My thoughts were scrambled as I moved through my morning routine on autopilot. Suddenly, I looked up and found myself parked in my Pop's driveway. I sighed and dropped my head against the steering wheel. This was the place I always ended up when my life made no sense.

Begrudgingly, I made my way to the front door and knocked. He opened the door, blinking blearily at the bright morning light.

"The cows aren't even awake yet, boy, what are you doing here?" he grumbled, stepping aside so I could come in.

When he saw my face, he immediately softened and clapped a hand on my shoulder.

"Let's get some coffee in me, and then we'll talk, yeah?"

After we'd settled ourselves at the kitchen table, he proceeded to stare at me while he sipped his coffee. I knew he was waiting for me to say something. I wasn't sure where to start.

"I'm retired, I've got all day," Pops chuckled. "You've got a business to run, so you'd better fess up quick before this trip is costing you money."

"Addy left." The words burned like fire in my throat.

Pops watched me before taking a long draw of his coffee. "Did she say why?"

I nodded. "But it doesn't make any sense. She was talking about her being a burden to me and wanting to give me space to decide whether I wanted to still be with her or not. Of course, I want to be with her, I've been telling her that since the day we met. I thought we were on the same page, so why would she suddenly think that I don't?"

"This have anything to do with her helping the cops catch that bastard?"

I winced. "We haven't actually talked about that lately. I kind of avoided that topic of conversation."

"So, what have you been talking to her about?"

I thought back over the last few weeks since she'd come home from the hospital.

"Her recovery, how she's feeling. I've been taking care of her, making sure she was taking her medicine, eating, doing her physical therapy, stuff like that."

Pops nodded and took another sip before turning a thoughtful look my way. "Is that it?"

"What do you mean?"

"Well, women need to feel validated, son," he said solemnly. I tried not to scoff. This man hadn't had a steady woman in his life since my mom left. Who was he to suddenly be the expert?

"Have you told her you love her lately? Have you said the words, 'I want to be with you no matter what happens'? I know you haven't talked about this thing she's setting up with the cops, which won't be easy for her. Think about what she's been going through. Squaring up to face a man who's put her in the hospital twice, all because she thinks there's a chance it'll help other women? She's got to be terrified, and all you've been talking to her about is her recovery?"

I could have hit myself. How had I not seen it?

"What the hell is wrong with me?" I moaned. "I know that this isn't going to be easy for her. But it's not easy for me either. What if something goes wrong? I can't lose her, Pops."

He reached out and patted my arm comfortingly. "I know, son. I know you're scared too, but she needs you right now. And you focused on protecting yourself in case something happens by pulling away. I've watched you do it your whole life."

"Of course she'd think she was a burden on me," I sighed.

Her words were seared into my brain, and they were only now making sense.

"She was trying to give me an out, in case I wanted to leave, because I've done nothing over the last few weeks to convince her that I'm not going anywhere. Even if I don't agree with her decision, I told her I'd be there for her through anything. I promised."

"Sounds like you've got some work to do to make good on that promise, then," Pops said with a soft smile.

I nodded and looked at my dad, more grateful than ever to have him in my life.

He watched me for a moment and then smacked my shoulder. "What are you still doing here? Go sort your shit, boy."

I laughed as I grabbed my car keys. I had a lot of apologizing to do, and I knew just the way to do it.

***

The Bell Tower was quiet as I made up our table in the corner of the restaurant. I was going to recreate the night we'd first confessed our love for each other. I was getting everything set up, and then I was going to call Addy and ask her to meet me here for dinner.

I'd closed the restaurant for the day. Greg wasn't thrilled, but he understood the need for a grand gesture. I'd hired the same jazz band that had been playing that night for a private concert for the two of us, and I was planning on spending all night with Addy in my arms. After, of course, I'd apologized profusely and explained why I'd been pulling away.

I set the last of the candles up and looked around. I'd really outdone myself, and pride bloomed in my chest.

I pulled out my phone to call Addy, and when I turned toward the door, I saw a disheveled looking man staring daggers at me through the window.

His hair was long and stringy, his eyes sunk deep into his skull, and his lips were snarled as he stared me down. It took a moment for me to realize he looked exactly as Addy had described Derek.

Anger raged through me as I raced to the door, but by the time I threw it open all I saw was the taillights of a beat up Camaro racing down the street away from the restaurant.

I growled to myself and decided that it was time to pay

199

Detective Harold a visit.

This bastard needed to rot in hell, and I was determined to make that happen.

Chapter Twenty-One

Addy

My breath was shaky as I finished the light jog around the trail. The doctor had said that I needed to start slowly when it came to physical activity, but that jogging was a good option to get my lungs back in shape. So here I was, forcing myself to keep my pace slow and steady.

I passed the bench where Bell had pretended to be my boyfriend to get those creepy guys to back off, and a different pain blossomed in my chest.

I hadn't seen or heard from him since I'd left the apartment to go to my parent's a few days ago. It was the longest we'd gone without talking since the diner incident.

I closed my eyes as they burned with unshed tears. I couldn't understand why he wouldn't just tell me we were done. I'd left that door open for him, given him the perfect out. And yet, nothing.

I shook my head, trying to forget about Bell for a moment. I had bigger things to worry about today.

I was meeting Detective Harold at the precinct to finalize the details of the plan. Checking my watch, I realized I'd be late if I didn't leave now.

The precinct wasn't anything special, a brown brick building in the middle of town. It hadn't been updated since probably the late eighties, and because we weren't a huge town there was a relaxed air in the place.

My sting operation was the most exciting thing to happen to these cops in years, and as I was led through the bullpen to the conference room, I could feel the buzz of peoples' whispers.

Detective Harold was kind as ever.

"Please have a seat, Ms. Jones," she smiled warmly, and the little ball of tension that had been building all morning eased a bit. "Would you like anything to drink? Coffee, water, juice?"

"Do you have any teas?"

"Of course, any special requests?"

"No, no, whatever you have is fine, thank you."

My fingers thrummed nervously against my knee. Detective Harold took a seat next to me and placed her hand lightly on mine.

"Everything is going to be fine, Ms. Jones. We've got a whole team of people, including S.W.A.T from the neighboring county, that are going to make sure that nothing happens to you. Derek Johnson will go away for the rest of his life, thanks to you."

That reminder of why I had agreed to this helped dispel the last of the nerves.

I squared my shoulders and looked into the detective's warm brown eyes. Bell's eyes were warm like hers, and a pang shot through my chest.

"Okay," I finally said. "Let's get to work then."

***

"Repeat the plan back to me," Detective Harold instructed me.

We'd been in the conference room for hours. Various people had filtered in and out to explain the different intricacies of the technological and tactical aspects of the operation. Detective Harold had made me repeat the plan about ten times now, and I was really hoping this would be the last one.

"On Tuesday next week I'll call Derek on the number I have for him from two years ago, which you've checked and is still connected. Whether he answers or not, I'll tell him that I need to talk to him.

"I'll say that I noticed how strung out he looked, and that I'm worried about him. I'll ask him to meet me, and I'll let him pick the meeting spot, so that he's more comfortable. He won't be able to resist seeing me, we hope.

"Once I know the spot, I'll text you and let you know, and then I'll go to the coffee shop on Main Street and meet Detective Kirby, who will set me up with a wire and a panic button.

"Then, I'll go to the meet, and as soon as I see Derek and confirm it's him, I hit the panic button and you'll be there in sixty seconds and arrest him. Then…it's over."

Detective Harold searched my face before smiling softly. "Perfect. All of this, what you're doing, is so brave, Ms. Jones. So many women will get the justice they deserve thanks to you."

I looked down at my hands and recited what I'd been saying since the hospital.

"I couldn't live with myself if he hurt someone else and I could've stopped him. Anyone would do what I'm doing, if they were in this situation."

"No, they wouldn't," Detective Harold was serious. "Very few people would put themselves in harm's way for the sake of strangers that they've never met."

Our eyes locked, and I was suddenly blinking back tears. My

thoughts went back to Bell standing up to defend me the night we met. The only one in a crowd of people to stop someone from doing something bad. My heart ached.

The detective patted my arm. "It'll all be over soon. Why don't you head home, and I'll call you tomorrow if any part of the plan changes."

***

As I stood outside of the police station waiting for my cab, a feeling of guilt washed over me.

Bell should know when it was happening. He had been against me doing it from the beginning, but he'd also taken really good care of me through my recovery, and we hadn't officially broken up.

Okay, and I was weak and wanted to talk to him.

Taking a few deep breaths, I dialed him. The line rang a few times, and then went to voicemail.

Anger, hot and heady, flashed through me.

If his phone was dead, it wouldn't have rung.

If he hadn't been with his phone, it would have rung longer and then went to voicemail.

But three rings? He'd declined my call.

I almost didn't leave a message, but the guilty feeling overpowered the anger. I blew out a long breath and tried to corral my tone into somewhere near polite.

"Hi Bell, it's me. I just wanted to let you know that -"

A hand twisted in my hair and yanked my head back, causing me to drop the phone. Before I could process what was happening, a cloth was pressed over my nose, and the world went dark.

204

Chapter Twenty-Two

Bell

Addy's name flashed across my phone, but I had to decline it. I was driving like a bat out of hell towards the police station and had to keep my concentration.

Seeing Derek through that window had sent a pit straight into my stomach. Something was seriously off with that man.

Anger and anxiety swirled through my blood, mixing with the adrenaline that had flared when I'd tried to chase him down. Fucker was fast. But he wouldn't be fast enough for Addy.

Her image flashed across my mind. Her dark curls glimmering red in the sunshine, her eyes sparkling as she looked at me with wonder. I didn't deserve to be loved by someone as amazing as her. I'd fucked everything up.

Now, I had to make it right.

My truck screeched to a stop in the parking lot as I threw it in park and raced into the building. I blew past the desk clerk and made my way up to the third floor where I knew the detectives' bullpen was.

I'd been somewhat of a troublesome youth, and before I'd gotten serious about going to college and doing something with myself, I'd been brought into Hartworth PD a few times.

There was an older Sargeant, Hitchins, who had finally sat me down and forced me to face reality.

"The only person you're punishing by acting out right now, is yourself," he'd said. "But keep this up, and eventually your actions will have consequences beyond you. You'll end up hurting somebody. So sharpen up before you do something you can't take back."

He was gruff and straightforward, but his words had broken through the wall of anger and hatred and self-righteousness that had fueled most of my decisions back then.

He'd saved me from myself. Something even Pops couldn't do, though Lord knows he'd tried.

As I made my way through the crowds of desks, I realized that the precinct was more alive than I'd ever seen it.

Hartworth wasn't all that big. Big enough that, yeah, I didn't know everybody in town, but not big enough to warrant the undercurrent of electricity that had seemed to have woken everybody up.

I finally spotted Detective Harold coming out of a conference room. She had stacks of folders in her hands and was moving quickly, as though she was in a hurry. Her face though, was calm and collected.

"Detective Harold," I called, picking up my pace to intercept her.

"Mr. Hawthorne," she sounded surprised. "What can I help you with?"

"I saw him." I was out of breath and had to take a moment to collect myself.

"Saw who?"

"Derek."

Her eyes sharpened and her hands tightened almost imperceptibly on the folders.

"Where?"

"Outside of my restaurant in downtown. I raced over here to tell you, in case it helped with anything."

"Thank you," she said. "Did you call Addy?"

"No." Unease trickled down my spine. "She called me when I was on my way here, but I didn't answer."

"She should know this," Detective Harold said, her eyes darting towards the doors. "She just left, we could probably still catch her."

"She's here?"

"I'm surprised you didn't pass her," Harold said, watching me closely.

The unease turned into ice.

I whipped my phone out of my pocket and dialed Addy.

It rang.

And rang. And rang.

She wasn't picking up.

Addy always picked up her phone. Even when she was at work. There had never been a time that I'd called that she hadn't answered. I knew we'd been going through a rough patch, but she'd *just* called me.

My gaze found Detective Harold', and she immediately read the panic in my eyes.

She picked up her radio and spoke into it clearly.

"Harold to front desk, do you have eyes on a late twenties brunette, curly hair, wearing a beige sweater and blue jeans?"

Static sounded for a moment before, "Copy Detective. The young woman exited the building about five minutes ago."

"Did you see where she went?"

"Negative."

I took off.

The elevator was too slow, so I raced down the stairs, bursting into the waiting area. I didn't slow as I slammed through the front doors, my eyes scanning everywhere for Addy.

Finally, they caught a glimpse of light in the bark next to the sidewalk.

I ran over and saw that it was a phone. I picked it up, my fingers shaking as I pressed the lock button and the screen lit up.

It was a picture of us. She'd taken it when we were curled up on Raelynn's couch after another game night. Her infectious smile stabbed my heart and my hands went numb. I didn't know where she was, but she would never have left her phone.

Detective Harold finally caught up to me, and her quick mind put together the pieces faster than I did.

"When she called you, did she leave a message?" the detective asked.

I blinked at her, my brain refusing to process new information.

Addy was gone. It was my fault. I hadn't been here for her. To keep her safe. To protect her.

"Mr. Hawthorne," Harold' voice was sharp, pulling me back.

"I don't know," I mumbled.

I checked my phone and sure enough there was a message from Addy.

"Hi Bell, it's me." She was annoyed. She must have known I'd hung up on her.

"I just wanted to let you know that –" she cut off and her words were replaced by a muffled scream.

The phone clattering to the ground ended the message. I stared at the useless brick in my hand, my vision dimming.

"He took her." My voice was low, the rage barely contained.

"We don't know that for certain," the detective was trying to placate me, but nothing was going to change what I knew.

"Look at the facts, Detective," I snapped, turning on her. "I see that scumbag outside of my restaurant and he takes off. He makes it here in the time that it takes me to close down and start driving. Addy calls me, because for some godforsaken reason she still has feelings for me. I don't pick up, because I'm racing here and can't afford a ticket for reckless driving. In that time, he took her."

Detective Harold watched me carefully, her eyes deep and knowing.

She held out her hand.

"I'll need your phone as evidence," she said softly. "We'll start working on tracking her down right now. He won't have her for long."

I handed over my phone and she turned, quickly marching back into the building.

My heart clawed its way into my throat as my mind spun.

If I had been two minutes earlier, I would have seen her. Or at least seen him dragging her off. Because I knew Addy, and she would have fought and screamed and defended herself until her last breath. Unless he'd drugged her.

My breathing was ragged as I pictured her, lifeless and limp, bruises covering her face and arms.

I wanted to scream. I wanted to hit something. I wanted to kill the man that had caused so much pain and suffering to so many people.

Addy didn't deserve this. She must be so scared. I had to show her. I had to show her that I would always be there for her.

I had to find her.

Chapter Twenty-Two

Addy

My head was pounding. I was so sick of that.

That was my first thought as I came to.

My second was that my arms were bent at an outrageously uncomfortable angle.

My third was that I shouldn't move.

I kept my breathing even, my head drooped onto my chest, and my eyes closed. And I listened.

There was a breeze that was swirling the loose hair on my face, tickling me. The air was musty and stale and smelled slightly of motor oil and cigarettes. Not an intelligent combination. A trickle of water echoed, making me think I was in a large space.

Rough rope bit into my wrists and ankles, and when I shifted my leg, cold metal burned my skin.

"I know you're awake," Derek's harsh voice said from my right.

I sighed and lifted my head, opening my eyes and taking in my situation.

I was in some sort of abandoned warehouse type building. Broken windows were badly boarded, letting in the breeze that swirled the dust through the air. As my eyes tried to focus, they could only track the particles of dirt that wound around my head. Finally, they focused and I saw the whole scenario. I was tied to an old metal chair that dug into my thighs and back.

My arms were crisscrossed around the back of the chair and tied to the sides, explaining the nagging ache in my shoulders. My ankles were bound with thick, scratchy rope that cut into my skin when I moved. My mouth tasted like cotton and my head was pounding.

I was in so much pain, but I didn't want to let Derek know that, so I took a deep breath and compartmentalized. I was good at that.

I focused on my anger, on the white-hot rage that was boiling inside of me, and the pain moved to the periphery of my problems.

"What the actual fuck, Derek?" I snarled, whipping my head around when he came out from behind me.

"You were helping the cops," he said. There was no malice in his voice, just pain and a little panic. "I couldn't let you turn me in, Ads."

"So, you kidnapped me?" I shook my head. "The drugs must've really corroded your brain, because this is just stupid. I'm back at work, I'm staying with my parents. People will notice that I'm gone, and who do you think the first person they're going to suspect is?"

"I sent an email to your boss saying you needed some more time to rehab, and I emailed your mom saying you were going back to your apartment," he said, almost guiltily.

The tiny spark of hope that had been in my chest flickered out.

My boss wouldn't question a last-minute time off request because she knew what was going on in my life.

My mom would think that I was going back to reconcile with Bell.

Bell...Bell who hadn't spoken to me in two days. Bell who had declined my call. Bell who wanted to break up with me, but couldn't figure out how to tell me. Bell who probably wouldn't even listen to the voicemail I'd left.

Nobody would know where I was until Detective Harold couldn't get a hold of me next Monday. Five days from now.

I watched Derek as he paced in front of me. His fingers twitched, and every few minutes he swatted at something invisible in front of him.

His hair was long, greasy, tangled, and matted, swishing along his back like ropes. His nails were dirty and jagged, and he kept biting them.

But it was his eyes that terrified me.

They were hollow, flitting around the room, not resting on anything because they weren't really seeing.

He was empty. A shell of the person that I'd once known. Seeing his eyes told me there was no soul to keep him in check anymore.

I wouldn't last five days. He'd kill me before then.

***

Derek left me alone for almost an entire day. The sunlight that streamed through the window told me how much time had passed, along with the cold that had crept into my fingers and toes and taken up residence there. On the bright side, I was slowly starting to lose feeling in my limbs, so soon the cold wouldn't be a problem.

When Derek came back, he lifted a bottle of water to my lips and ended up pouring half of it down the front of me.

"What the fuck, Derek?" I gasped.

"Shut the fuck up and be grateful I thought about water at all," he grumbled.

I blinked.

Earlier he'd been apologetic, frantic. Now he was stone-faced and angry, his energy vibrating like a chihuahua in December. I didn't want to make him mad. I remembered his temper all too well.

I took a deep breath to calm myself.

"I'm sorry for snapping. Thank you for the water," I said softly.

He looked at me for a long moment. His empty eyes swept down my body in a way that used to light my skin on fire, but now made me nauseous.

"Finally, some gratitude," he growled. "You know, I can think of better ways for you to thank me."

He stalked over to me and ran a disgustingly long fingernail along my cheek. I shuddered and twisted my face away from him.

Hot anger flickered across his face, the first real emotion I'd seen from him so far, and my mouth went dry.

His hand wrapped around my chin and yanked it back towards him. His breath was rancid in my nose as he brought our mouths an inch apart.

"You think you're fucking better than me, bitch?" he snarled. His fingernails cut into my cheeks, and fear made my heart pound.

I thought it would be better if I didn't say anything, but that was also a bad idea, as he growled low in his throat and crushed his mouth against mine. When I struggled against his grip, his other hand wrapped around my throat and squeezed. His tongue raked against my lips, and I snarled away from him.

That did it. He pulled back and brought his fist across my cheek.

Blood surged into my mouth and dripped down my chin as pain blossomed behind my eyes.

"You're not better than me, Ads," he said, his voice dripping acid. "I'll remind you one more time, yeah?"

I started to shake my head when another blow landed on the

other cheek. I felt blood drip down my face and knew he'd broken the skin (and possibly the bone) with that hit.

Tears welled in my eyes, and my breathing was rasping as I tried not to swallow the blood in my mouth. I let my head hang limply, refusing to meet his gaze so that I wouldn't antagonize him more.

He took a deep breath and stood back. I felt him watching me, and I couldn't help the tears that rolled down my cheeks, hot and stinging against the cuts.

I hated feeling weak. I had promised myself that I would never be weak again. But tied to this chair, blood dripping down my cheek, I was powerless.

He laughed low in his throat.

"I've waited so long to see you like this, Ads," he admitted.

He circled and when he was behind me, he twisted his hand in my hair and yanked my head up. His lips were at my ear.

"Completely at my mercy. No fight left in you. Just the way I like it."

Bile rose in my throat as anger flooded through me. I suddenly knew exactly how all of those women must have felt.

Had he beat them into submission? Had he made them bleed until they were too exhausted to fight, and then taken whatever he wanted from them?

I wasn't weak. I wasn't powerless. And I sure as hell wasn't letting him take anything from me without a fight.

Acting on pure rage, I slammed the side of my head into his nose. I felt hot liquid spurt onto my hair as Derek howled in pain. His grip on my hair loosened, and I took the chance to bounce my chair backwards into him, knocking him to the floor.

Adrenaline pumped through me as I took in Derek holding his face on the ground. I looked at the door and knew I had one chance.

214

I bounced my chair across the floor, racing as quickly as I could towards the light. I was screaming my lungs out. My limbs were so numb, and in my adrenalized state I registered shock that they were even working.

But I knew I wasn't going to make it.

Derek was on his feet, racing after me. I sensed him behind me and did the only thing I could think of. I threw myself sideways just as he jumped, and as I landed on my side I rolled as much as I could so that the legs of the chair were sticking in the air.

Derek landed squarely on one of the legs, bending it with his weight. It knocked the air out of him and broke a rib judging from the sputters of pain that came from him.

I let my body sink into the floor, panting and wincing at the painful angle of my limbs with the weight of the chair keeping me on the ground.

The only solace I had from my failed escape attempt was that I'd managed to hurt Derek just as badly as he'd hurt me.

We both lay on the ground for a long time, and I was starting to worry I'd never have the use of my limbs again when he groaned and stood over me.

His nose was swollen and bent, his eyes blossoming with fresh bruises, and he was clutching his right side.

"You stupid bitch," he spat, bloody spittle sticking to my skin.

He yanked me up, setting the chair on the now uneven legs and then dragging me to the back wall. He pulled a chain from under a work bench and twisted it around my torso, around the back of the chair, and then looped it through an exposed pipe. He secured it with an industrial lock.

He stood back to admire his work with a broken smirk on his bleeding face. Then his eyes found mine, and all I saw was darkness.

***

The next few hours of my life were literal torture. When Derek was satisfied that he'd at least broken a few of my fingers and ribs, he had pulled a pocketknife out and taken time to trace thin lines down my thigh. Whenever I cried out, he laughed.

The only thing that kept me alive was thinking about Bell.

I disappeared into a corner of my mind and spent the hours snuggled under the blankets with him. Tracing nonsense patterns across his chest. Listening to his honey-smooth voice. Feeling the little zaps of lightning that always raced down my skin whenever he touched me.

I replayed conversations, made up new ones. I told him how sorry I was for not just talking to him. For being such a burden. I told him how much I loved him. How grateful I was that he hadn't given up on me.

Derek was out of his mind, consumed with hate and heroin. He tried his best to break me, to drag me into his darkness. But I held on tightly to my personal sun god, and somehow made it through.

When Derek finally started to come down from the high he'd been on, he looked at me like he was going to be sick.

"Ads, did I …" he trailed off, horror flashing across his face.

I was too weak to respond, focusing my energy on my next breath through the pain of broken ribs. At least I was still breathing, which meant that he hadn't perforated a lung. A dry chuckle rasped from my throat as I thought how lucky I must be.

When I managed to lift my eyes to his, he was crying, tears tracing tracks down his bloodstained face. When our eyes locked, his widened, and then he turned and ran out of the warehouse.

As soon as he was gone, tears of my own were winding down my cheeks, because just for a moment I'd seen the Derek that I'd

216

been so in love with. And that Derek was heartbroken at what he'd just done.

Soon, my tears turned into sobs that wracked painfully through my body. I don't know if it was the pain, the exhaustion, or the last of my willpower crumbling, but eventually my eyes closed and I drifted into a painless sleep.

***

I don't know how long I slept, but when Derek threw icy water on my face to wake me the sunlight was filtering red through the broken windows.

I squeezed my eyes together as the pain returned to my body.

"Please…"

The broken word escaped my lips before I could stop it.

A manic grin flashed across Derek's face, and he knelt so that he could look at my face without me having to lift my head.

"Please what, baby?" he purred. As soon as his breath fanned across my face, I knew what was coming next.

"Please, let me go." I tried anyway.

He chuckled darkly and swept his knuckles along my bruised cheekbone.

"I can't let you go, Ads," he said seriously. "I love you."

I scoffed, hatred spewing from deep inside me. He was going to kill me either way, and I was done trying to stop him.

"This isn't love, jackass. Love is selfless, and protective, and soothing. Loving another person takes everything inside of you, and you still don't feel like you're giving enough, but you know you'll always keep trying to give them more. And being loved by another person fills you.

"When you can accept that love, it spreads throughout your

entire body, taking away all of the pain and sadness and replacing it with warmth and light. Even when you fuck up, you know that person will still love you, because they've promised to love every part of you, not just the parts they cherry pick. Because they know that you'll love all of them, all of the darkness and all of the light, together.

"You don't know what love is. Because you've never loved me. And I've never loved you. Not really."

"You think you're so smart?" Derek snarled, his fingers twisting the collar of my shirt and yanking it down over my shoulder. He bit down hard on the skin of my collarbone, and I gritted my teeth against the pain. "You think that giant dickhead loves you? Then where is he? You called and left him a message. Where is he, Adelaide? Hmm?"

I bit the inside of my cheek. I would never stop loving Bell, and it hurt to have the fact that he wasn't talking to me thrown back in my face.

Especially from someone who could never possibly understand what I'd felt when I was with Bell. How pure that love had been.

I looked into Derek's eyes, hating the way they slithered over my body like he owned me. I wanted him to stop that look, so I said the only thing I knew to be true in that moment.

"Bell is right here with me," I muttered softly. "He's in every part of me, every cell, every breath, every beat of my heart. And you can never take him away from me."

Something unearthly and sinister grew in Derek's answering smile.

"You think so? How about I brand you. Leave a mark so deep that you'll have me in every cell, breath, and heartbeat for the rest of your miserable fucking life. How about that?"

My lips trembled as I took in the cold distance and evil in his eyes.

Then, he flashed a wicked smile and ripped my top off of my shoulder, exposing my bra. His hands trailed down to my jeans, where he unbuttoned them and yanked them down my legs.

With my arms tied, I was powerless to stop him. My muscles strained to use all of the techniques I had been practicing for years. Moves that would incapacitate him. My soul itched to show him that I wasn't powerless. That I was strong. That he couldn't take away my will to live.

His hands forced my legs apart. I closed my eyes as my stomach heaved, knowing what he was about to do, and resigning myself to my fate.

His hands were reaching for his belt when he suddenly froze. I looked at him, trying to figure out what was going on, when all hell broke loose.

Lights blared, sirens wailed, and dozens of men in dark tactical gear flooded the warehouse.

Derek was thrown to the ground. Detective Harold stood triumphantly over him as a uniformed officer put him in cuffs and read him his rights.

And suddenly he was just… gone.

Rough hands undid the ropes at my wrists and ankles.

A bolt cutter removed the chain around my torso.

Paramedics rushed me.

Hands touched my face, my wrists, my stomach.

A blanket wrapped protectively around me.

A stretcher appeared.

Then the warehouse was behind me. I craned my neck to take a last look at a place I hoped would burn.

When I looked forward, through the flashing lights, the thrum of bodies, the oxygen mask on my face, my entire world narrowed.

Bell.

Standing next to Detective Harold, he was aggravated. Then, as if he could feel my gaze on him, he looked up and our eyes locked.

The detective was mid-sentence when Bell ran away from her. To me.

He barreled to the stretcher, and the paramedics stopped. He came to a halt a foot from me, his eyes searching my face, tears streaming down his.

Then, ever so gently, I reached out and touched his wrist. His gaze dropped to my fingers, came back to my eyes, and then he choked on a sob.

"I thought I'd lost you," he cried.

I heard my own cries as I clutched his wrist with all my strength.

The paramedics said something, and luckily Bell was cognizant enough to hear them. My heart was pounding in my ears, and my vision was black on the edges, focused only on the man standing next to me.

Then, we were moving. Into the ambulance, Bell climbing into the back, his hand never leaving mine.

They hooked up an IV, and the last thing I saw before the darkness was Bell's sparkling face. I knew that they were tears, but through the drugs I could have sworn I saw him glowing, halo and all.

Chapter Twenty-Three

Addy

"You need to stay in bed, Miss Jones," the nurse said, gently pushing my shoulder until I sank back into the pillows.

"No, I need to walk around so I can get out of here sooner," I grumbled under my breath.

She'd heard me and chuckled softly. "You're already healing much faster than we'd hoped, so how about a little patience? Let's not push your body too far too fast, okay?"

"Listen to your nurse, Addy." Bell's voice rang from the doorway.

He was leaning against the doorframe, a small coffee cup in his hands and a smirk on his lips.

"Yes, sir," I said sarcastically.

I didn't miss the arousal that flitted across his face and smiled to myself when he quickly schooled his expression to one of mild annoyance.

The nurse smiled to herself while she checked my vitals. Bell made his way to the chair that he'd been occupying the entirety of my now two week long stay in the hospital.

He'd barely been home, just once every few days to shower,

and he was never gone more than an hour at a time. The first night the nurses had tried to remove him after visiting hours ended, Detective Harold had to intervene. Bell was allowed to stay nights after that.

Which was good, because we'd had a lot to talk about.

Turns out, Bell had ignored my call because he was driving to the police station to ask Detective Harold how he could help.

He'd said that even two days apart were misery for him. He'd tried to figure out why I left, and apparently it took a trip to see his dad for the pieces to fall into place.

Once they did, he'd realized that he hadn't been showing me that he wanted to be with me, he'd been distant. I'd told him that I thought I was doing what was best – setting him free, so that he didn't feel obligated to keep taking care of me. Once he'd realized that he needed to show me that he would do anything to keep me in his life, he'd planned a romantic night for us at The Bell Tower, where he was going to show me how much I meant to him and apologize.

He was going to offer to come with me to the planning sessions. He was going to show me that he wasn't going anywhere. And it was at the restaurant setting up that he'd seen Derek watching him, and he knew he needed to report it.

When he'd arrived at the station, Detective Harold was confused, saying that he should have passed me coming into the building, as I'd just left. They'd found my phone in the bushes out front. That's when Bell had checked his phone and listened to the partial voicemail.

When they'd realized what happened, the entire precinct sprang into action. They dug into everything they knew about Derek. They hunted down associates, old addresses, past victims, and eventually they learned that Derek had been fired from an auto parts processing warehouse that had since shut down. It took them two days, but they found me. Just in time.

Detective Harold had been to visit a few days into my stay with good news.

Derek had given a full confession, and would be pleading guilty to aggravated assault, aggravated sexual assault, kidnapping, and possession with the intent to distribute. She said he was looking at a double life sentence, with no option of parole.

That made focusing on healing a lot easier, and Bell was by my side through every part of it. From the days where just sitting up in bed had me in tears, to the days all I wanted was to walk down to the cafeteria and get some ice cream.

As I started to feel better, he'd climb into the hospital bed with me as I fell asleep, holding me tightly to him. It was there, in his arms, in the moment before I fell asleep, that a little voice would pop into my head. This little voice said the same thing, every night.

I want to marry this man.

***

"So, how are you processing?"

Dr. Laura sat on my couch next to me. We were in my apartment, curled up under blankets with hot mugs of tea steaming on the coffee table. I was still in recovery, and going out was too difficult for me, so Bell had insisted on Laura coming to me to help me through the mental recovery.

My hand curled over the scars on my thigh and I took a breath. "It's day by day, honestly. Some days I feel fine. I can function and interact with people and feel normal. Other days...other days I can barely open my eyes because the memories overwhelm me. But those days are getting less and less.

"I've been journaling a lot, one of your suggestions, and it helps to just write whatever is in my head to get it out. I should be cleared for starting small physical activity next week, so I'll be able to get back to my exercise routine, which I think will help."

"It's going to be a long road, Addy," Laura said. She'd been telling me this every session since the hospital. I knew that she wanted to set my expectations, but I had a feeling she was reminding herself, too.

"I know, and I'm prepared for that. I'm ready to do the work," I smiled. "I have a better support system now than I had the first time, which is good because this was...worse. Much worse, much more traumatic, obviously. But I have Bell, who I didn't have before, and he's made more of a difference than I would've thought."

"How are things between you and Bell?"

"Honestly, they're also day by day," I laughed softly. "Not in any kind of bad way, but because everything is still pretty fresh there are days when I need Bell more than I need air, and there are other days that it's hard to be around him. But he hasn't left, and even on the really bad days he gives me my space but makes sure that I know that he's here if I need him. He increased his own sessions with his therapist, which is helping him work through this without dumping it all on me, which I appreciate."

"That all sounds very healthy," Laura nodded.

"I love him so much," I sighed.

My eyes widened as I realized I hadn't yet spoken to her about what I wanted to ask Bell.

"Laura, what does marriage mean to you?"

"To me as a woman or to me as your therapist?"

"Both? Tell me what it means to you personally first, then I want to hear what it means to you as a therapist."

She looked at me thoughtfully for a moment before twisting the golden band on her finger.

"My wife is my best friend. She's my partner, in every sense of the word. She is always honest with me, and she grounds me. She and I know that we can tell each other anything, and that we can continue to grow as human beings with each other. I can't imagine my life without her, even in the most difficult times.

"For me, as a woman, marriage is finding your harbor in a storm. Someone who makes you feel safe and loved. As your therapist, I know that thinking of being with one person for the rest of your life can be daunting. It's a promise of trust. It's a promise of being there for the other person as they go through the trials and tribulations of their life, leaving room for them to continue to grow. Marriage says, 'I am choosing to love every version of you for the rest of our time here.' And that's a pretty powerful statement to make."

She watched me for a moment and then reached out to pat my knee.

"You aren't a flippant person, Addy. You don't jump into things without thinking about them, so I have to ask, how long have you been thinking about marriage?"

I sighed. "Since the hospital. Maybe even before that. When I came out of that warehouse and saw Bell, it was like I was seeing my future. I saw so clearly that he was it for me. I don't want to give myself to anyone else, ever again. But I also know that I was in shock, and that I could just be feeling like this because Bell has been my savior over and over again throughout our relationship. So maybe I'm just clinging to him because he makes me feel safe?"

Laura nodded as if this made all the sense in the world, even though I thought I sounded insecure and a little pathetic.

"You are still recovering from a hugely traumatic event, Addy," she said kindly. "Now, I don't doubt that you and Bell are very much in love, after everything you've told me. But you also don't have to make any decisions right now. Focus on recovery, focus on building your life back up, focus on being in the moment with Bell. And keep talking. To him, to me, to whoever you want. I think that time will bring a lot of clarity."

I smiled and then winced when a sharp pain lanced through my chest. Time was exactly what I needed.

Chapter Twenty - Four

Addy

Four months later.

"Keep up, slowpoke!" I laughed as I heard Bell panting behind me.

I heard his low chuckle and then his footsteps falling even further behind me. I rolled my eyes and sprinted to the end of the trail, waiting as he slowly jogged to meet me.

Bell and I had been running together every Friday morning since I'd been cleared to start physical activity again. He'd been a bit miffed at my choice of activity, but we'd gotten back to our intimate rhythm pretty quickly after that.

Running with Bell was different. When I had started running after my first attack, it was a way to find solitude inside of my own mind. Focusing on the burn in my lungs and the ache in my legs had kept me from spinning out into panic attacks.

With Bell, I felt like we were sharing that peace. We didn't talk much on our runs, both of us using the time to process. And they had led to some truly amazing conversations in the car on the way home. Having time to collect our thoughts made them easier to face and articulate.

After one run, Bell had insisted that we install a home security system. He said that he would feel better if he knew I was safe when

I was home alone. He'd also asked if we could always share our locations with each other. That one completely made sense to me.

Even though Derek was in prison and would be for the rest of his natural life, there was always going to be a lingering fear.

I'd forgotten to charge my phone one day before I left for work, and in the fifteen-minute bus ride Bell had called seven times. When I'd finally made it to the office, he was just pulling up in a panic. Not knowing where I was or why I hadn't answered my phone had sent him into a full spiral.

After another run, I had confessed to Bell that I hated looking at myself in the mirror. My thighs were covered in thin scars, and whenever I caught a glimpse of my reflection I could only remember feeling so powerless in that chair.

Bell had sat with me in front of the mirror that night and had traced my entire body, telling me everything that he loved about each part of me. His legs had caged me in, and his arms had held me close to his chest, so that I couldn't move, and he'd made sure he was making eye contact with me as he monologued about various freckles and bumps and lines in my skin.

Running with Bell was good for both of us. It had opened up our lines of communication, which we'd desperately needed after the entire ordeal. I knew it wasn't his favorite activity, but he did it to be close to me. And he very much enjoyed the benefits of a post-run adrenaline high.

I shook my head to bring my thoughts back. The air was crisp and cold, and I could see my breath in front of me with every exhale.

Bell finally made it over to me and leaned in to give me a quick kiss.

"You were even slower than normal today," I teased.

"I couldn't make myself go any faster," he admitted.

I cocked my head. "And why is that? Are you feeling okay?"

He grinned and wrapped his arms around my waist, pulling my body close to his.

"I'm feeling just fine, darlin'. The view was just too good to pass up."

I felt heat rising to my cheeks as he gently pressed a kiss to my lips. He lingered, leaving me swaying and chasing the heat of his body when he finally pulled away with a smirk.

"Ten months together and I can still make you blush," he marveled.

"We could be together sixty years, and you'd still make me blush," I grumbled, pulling away from him so I could stretch.

"That sounds like a challenge to me," I heard him say under his breath.

I smiled to myself as I bent to stretch out my hamstrings. I felt Bell's eyes on me, but continued my stretch, trying to ignore the heat building in my chest.

I stood up and found that he was watching me with glazed eyes. I knew that look. It meant that his mind was a million miles away, and from the desire that flickered across his face I knew exactly what he was thinking. I snapped my fingers in front of his face and watched as he came back to the present moment.

"Don't get distracted," I playfully admonished him. "We've got a lot to get done today before the party at The Bell Tower, so focus up."

"Yes, ma'am." He did a mock salute before leaning in and stealing one more kiss.

I shook my head and turned away from him to avoid jumping into his arms. "Let's get back to the car."

"Before we go, I have something for you," he said. He sounded almost…shy?

That couldn't be right. Bell was a lot of things, but shy was not one of them.

I turned and saw him reaching into his fanny pack that he insisted on wearing on our runs. I'd told him he looked ridiculous. He maintained that he looked like a nineties era Dwayne Johnson. Either way, I had lost the battle when he rightfully pointed out that I would never know the pain of jogging with car keys in my pockets and having them hit the family jewels with each stride.

He pulled out a small notebook, no bigger than his palm.

It was tattered and clearly well-worn.

"This is an early Christmas present," he said.

He held the notebook tightly in his hands, as if he was afraid to let go of it. But, with a deep breath, he offered it to me.

"Thank you," I smiled up at him. "I don't have anything for you. All of your presents are under the tree at home."

"I know, I've counted them," he grinned at me.

I rolled my eyes and then looked down at the little book in my hands.

"What is this?"

"It's everything that I wanted to tell you when we weren't dating."

I blinked up at him, not fully comprehending.

"When we were friends," he explained, "I wrote down everything that I wanted to tell you but didn't think was appropriate to share with a friend. It was every thought, every feeling, every little moment that I would have shared with my girlfriend, but not my girl friend."

Tears pricked at my eyes as I stared at him.

"Why are you giving it to me now?" I whispered.

He shrugged, trying so hard to look nonchalant, but I knew this was important to him.

"I just thought it was time," he said. "I wanted you to have it for Christmas."

"Bell," I breathed, unsure what to say.

I flipped through the book and snippets flashed out at me.

You looked downright fuckable today.

I snorted a laugh. Of course, that would be the first one I saw.

Sometimes, when you're not looking, I try to memorize every freckle on your skin.

A lump formed in my throat, but I kept reading.

Maybe it was a good thing my mom left me. Because I know how it feels to be left behind, and I won't ever do that to you.

I flipped through a few more pages, fighting back tears.

I realized for the first time today that I'm in love with you. You were sitting across from me, and you took a sip of your tea and it was too hot. Instead of yelling or anything like that, you stuck your tongue out and tried to blow on your tongue to cool it off. It was adorable.

I looked up at him and couldn't stop the tears from sliding down my face.

"You kept these thoughts to yourself all that time?"

"I didn't want to scare you off," he admitted.

I sniffled and tucked the book against my chest, holding it tight. I looked up at him and was lost for words. How would I ever possibly be able to express the thousands of feelings that were cascading through me?

Our entire relationship, Bell had been watching me, learning everything that he could, even when I refused to tell him. Because he'd seen something in me that he knew he would love, and he wanted to unearth it. The entire time he was falling in love with me, I was trying so hard not to fall in love with him.

He'd been so patient. So sweet. So understanding.

A fresh set of tears fell, and he reached forward to cup my cheeks in his hands, gently brushing them off.

"If you *ever* think that I don't love you, I want you to read this journal and remember that I have always loved you. From the moment I saw you."

He waited for me to nod, still unable to speak. Then, the most brilliant smile broke out on his face and he captured my lips for a searing kiss. His arms settled around me and lifted me, and I swore he was lifting my very soul.

I didn't know how I could love this man any more than I did in that moment.

***

Raelynn and I were flicking through dresses, each looking for the perfect one for the restaurant's holiday party tomorrow night.

The Bell Tower had become our favorite place. It was like a second home for us, so it had only made sense that when Bell and Greg suggested throwing a holiday party for the employees, Raelynn and I had immediately offered to plan it.

We had bought all the decorations and had spent hours hanging lights and bits and bobs until the restaurant was a winter wonderland. We were excited to finally get to sit back and enjoy the spoils of our labors.

As a thank you, Bell had told us to go and buy ourselves dresses, on him, no limit.

There were many things to love about the man, but the way that he spoiled me was slowly worming its way higher.

I had been uncomfortable with it at first, but Bell didn't overdo it. He rarely bought me things, instead spoiling me with his affection and attention. So, when he had handed me his card and told me to have fun, I had promised him I would. Then he'd made me promise again, but told me to mean it that time. He knew me too well.

"What about this one?" Raelynn held up a pretty chiffon dress in a deep purple.

I looked at it, but it wasn't right. I shook my head and Raelynn laughed.

"You sure are making a big deal out of your boyfriend's Christmas party. You've been anal about everything being perfect from the beginning," she chuckled to herself.

"Well, if I have my way, after tomorrow night he'll be my fiancé," I smirked.

I felt Raelynn's gaze on my face, but I continued to shuffle through dresses.

"He's going to ask you to marry him?" she nearly squealed.

I pursed my lips, still concentrating on the clothing. "I don't know. I don't think so."

"Then why –"

"I'm going to ask him."

More silence. I felt her coming around the rack to stand next to me, but I kept my focus on the clothing. A gentle hand on my arm. When I finally looked at her, Raelynn's eyes were misty.

"You love him that much, you're sure?" she asked, her voice soft and compassionate.

"I can't imagine my life without him," I smiled, remembering

Laura's words when she'd talked about her wife. "And I can't wait another minute to have him as my husband."

Her face broke out in a massive smile and she hugged me tightly. Then, she suddenly pulled back, holding me at arm's length.

"He's not going to be upset that you're asking instead of him?"

I laughed. "No, Bell's not as fragile as that," I reassured her. "But I do want to look amazing, just to minimize the chances of him saying no."

It was Raelynn's turn to laugh. "That man can't say no to you for anything."

I bit my lip, knowing she was probably right, but feeling nerves settle in my stomach nonetheless.

We spent another hour looking at dresses, which was officially too much for me. I was just about to call it quits when we passed by a little boutique tucked in the corner of the mall.

I dragged Raelynn inside, and after two minutes found the perfect dress.

The fabric rippled through my fingers like water, and I knew I had to have it.

***

The Bell Tower was something else around Christmas time.

The dining space was decked out with three huge trees with all the trimmings. Popcorn and cranberries, twinkling lights, big bobble ornaments.

Bell had asked each of the staff members to decorate an ornament and they hung proudly on the biggest tree.

The walls glittered with colorful lights, and fake snow littered the rafters. Raelynn and I had hung icicle lights along the entire ceiling, creating the most beautiful, wintery atmosphere.

All of that was nothing compared to the beauty of the man that was escorting me around for introductions. His fitted dark suit hugged his waist and broad shoulders, his hair was freshly trimmed, and he was glowing.

The dress I'd landed on was a simple black satin number with a low back and deep V neckline. The skirt flirted with my knees, flaring whenever I turned just right. Bell's eyes had gone almost completely black when I'd walked out in it, so I knew it was the right choice.

Even though it was a staff-only party, the place was packed. Everyone had invited friends and family, and by seven o'clock the party was in full swing. People were laughing and drinking, chatting.

As one of the owners, Bell had an obligation to say hello to every single employee. Which meant saying hello to every single employee's guests.

He did it effortlessly. I could see the love that he had for his people with every conversation he had. He was so genuine, and I wondered if everybody else knew the depth of how incredible he was?

I, however, was not as social as the love of my life. After meeting so many people, I could feel my battery starting to drain. I needed to keep at least a bit of energy if the rest of the night went how I hoped it would.

I finally excused myself to sit at the bar with Raelynn and Johnny, letting Bell make his own rounds.

Watching Bell mingle and laugh with everybody was almost mesmerizing. He was genuinely excited and happy to talk with each and every person that wanted to talk with him. He was magnetic. And he was mine.

A familiar warmth tingled through me as I pictured what our

future would look like.

Wherever we ended up, whatever roads we took, I knew we would be fine because we would be together. Before Bell, my life had been about surviving one day to the next. Relearning how to be around people, how to move through my emotions and just…function. I had my stable job, my parents, and Raelynn, and that was all I could even imagine handling.

Then this hulking sweetheart of a man had melted all of my walls. He'd reintroduced me to someone I had forgotten I was. I still had piles of fears and insecurities and trauma to work through, but I wasn't afraid of it. I wasn't content with simply surviving anymore. I wanted to live. I wanted to experience life with Bell. To travel, and adventure with him. I wanted everything.

Johnny poured me a glass of champagne as we sat and watched the crowd. He and Raelynn kept sneaking kisses, and I deliberately ignored their plans to have a quickie in the storage room. I'd have to tell Bell to give it a good sanitization after the party.

"So, any plans for when you're going to ask him?" Raelynn finally asked with a playful nudge to my arm, forcing my gaze away from the actual Sun God that was my, hopefully, soon to be fiancé.

I felt heat creeping up my cheeks and glanced over to make sure Bell was still a good distance away.

"I was thinking of asking him after we got home tonight," I said nervously. "As long as neither of us has too much to drink that is. It's too important of a question to ask him if we're tipsy."

"I think it's cute that you're nervous, even though you *know* he's going to say yes," Raelynn laughed.

"Just because you proposed to Johnny on your living room floor and he said yes after three weeks of dating, doesn't mean it's going to work like that for me," I sighed.

I had been flabbergasted when she'd told me that. But it was so very Raelynn, that it hadn't surprised me for more than a moment. It had been more surprising that Johnny had said yes.

"Well, here's some of my unending confidence for you," Raelynn said as she rubbed her hands down my shoulders with a giggle.

I rolled my eyes and laughed along but couldn't shake the little seed of doubt in my stomach. It was a big ask, and even though I was ninety five percent sure Bell's answer would be yes, there was the other five percent that made me feel like throwing up.

Before I could say anything else, Bell appeared at my side.

"They're playing our song," he said softly in my ear, nodding at the jazz band in the corner.

They were playing the same song that I'd dragged Bell onto the dance floor for when I'd first told him I loved him. The same song that older couple had danced to, the ones who made me fall in love with The Bell Tower in the first place.

I grinned as Bell took my hand and led me to the dance floor, pulling my body close to his and humming along as we swayed.

I closed my eyes, reveling in the perfection of this moment. His arms around me felt so safe and strong, his body turning me now and then, leading me in a slow waltz around the room. The low buzz of conversation faded whenever I looked into his eyes. I rested my head on his chest as his hand settled in the small of my back, somehow drawing me even closer.

Suddenly, everything became so clear. This was the moment. It was perfect.

I pulled back to look at him and opened my mouth to speak just as he did the same. Our eyes locked and we laughed.

"You first," he said.

"No, you."

A smile swept across his face.

"Together?"

I took a deep breath and nodded.

He held up three fingers and slowly lowered them. When the last one was gone, we both spoke.

"Will you marry me?"

"What?"

We'd stopped moving and were holding on to each other tightly, simply staring at each other before we both broke out laughing.

His deep belly laugh sent warmth all the way to my toes, and tears pricked my eyes as my own laughter stole my breath.

I was dimly aware that the rest of the room was watching us curiously, having our laughing fit in the middle of the dance floor, but I couldn't seem to care as we each descended further into giggles.

When we were finally able to compose ourselves, our eyes locked. His were sparkling.

"So, is that a yes?" he asked.

I smirked. "That depends. Is it a yes from you?"

His eyes flashed and he pulled me roughly into him, one hand on my waist and the other tangling in my hair as he crashed our lips together.

When he finally pulled back, he rested his forehead against mine. "I'll always say yes to you, Addy."

"Forever?"

"Forever and ever, gorgeous."

The smile on my face was painful, but I couldn't have stopped it if I'd tried. I kissed him again as he lifted me in the air and spun me around. When he set me down, he reached into his back pocket and pulled out a little black box.

Inside was a beautiful, simple, gold band, thin with a small diamond in the center, and three smaller diamonds on each side. It looked vintage, and it was absolutely perfect. It also meant that we had been on the same page for awhile without ever actually telling the other. This was a ring that had taken time to find.

My heart swelled as he slipped it onto my finger and then kissed it.

The room broke out into applause, and we finally descended from the cloud we'd been on to look around at all of the smiling faces.

The rest of the night blurred into congratulations and champagne and dancing and laughter. When we finally made it home, we were both so exhausted that we collapsed into bed. I snuggled into his chest, my left hand resting on his stomach. He reached up and grabbed it, holding it up so that the diamond caught the light.

"If I wasn't so tired, I'd tie you up so that I could take you from behind and just stare at that ring as I came inside you," he said roughly.

I laughed even as a faint wave of arousal washed through me. "Ever the gentleman," I murmured into his chest. My eyes were heavy, and I was trying to stay awake.

"How about you take me in the morning, fiancé?" I managed to grumble.

I felt his laughter in his chest and then his lips on my hair. "That sounds perfect, fiancée."

Chapter Twenty- Five

Addy

It turned out that planning a wedding with Bell was the easiest thing in the world. Neither of us wanted a big wedding, just our family and friends. We didn't want to spend a lot of money on the wedding because we wanted to spend it on a long honeymoon to the Caribbean, so everything was simple.

Four months after we'd proposed to each other, we were back at The Bell Tower. The dining room had been transformed into a beautiful wedding venue. Chairs were lined up facing the small stage where the band usually sat, and they were draped in white linens. The bare light bulbs hanging from the ceiling glowed like floating lanterns in the air. The smell of magnolias wafted on the breeze.

I had been sequestered in the boys' office to get ready, while they prepared themselves in the backroom of the brewery.

"Are you ready for this?" Raelynn asked as she pinned my curls back.

I smiled at her in the mirror. "I've been ready for months."

Her gaze warmed and her hands rested on my shoulders.

"I've never seen you so sure about anything before," she said. "It's nice. You seem…settled."

"I am," my voice was soft.

"Bell is a good man."

That was an understatement. Before I could answer her, Justine came into the room with three glasses and a bottle of champagne.

"Okay, let's cut the sappy crap," she said in the crisp, no-nonsense way she was famous for. "The bride needs a drink to take the edge off."

"I don't have an edge," I laughed.

"Then just humor me," she deadpanned.

Two glasses of champagne and three full faces of makeup later, my mom poked her head in to let us know it was time to go.

Justine, Raelynn, and I made our way out of the office and walked down the short hallway that separated it from the main dining area. I could hear the music switch to the slow and sweet violin piece we'd picked, and the chatter of our guests die down.

Justine gave me a quick smile and then turned the corner.

"Three deep breaths," Raelynn said, wrapping me in a tight hug before she too was gone.

I had initially felt bad not inviting either of my parents to walk me down the aisle, but I knew this was something I needed to do on my own. After everything I had been through, making this choice of ultimate trust was for me and me alone.

First breath. The violin began the bridal march.

Second breath. I heard the guests shuffle to their feet.

Third breath.

The doors opened and I was staring across the room into the eyes of the love of my life.

Bell's face broke out into a heartbreaking grin and tears rolled down his cheeks. My pulse hammered in my ears, and I couldn't stop the wide smile that took over me.

I have no recollection of telling my feet to move or trying to match the pace of the song. There was only one thought in my head, and that was *I need to be married to this man right now.*

By the time I finally made it to the end of the aisle, my cheeks were coated with my own tears, and Bell was reaching out to take my hand. The warmth of his skin settled my racing heart. Everything quieted as we drank each other in.

Our eyes never left each other as the pastor recited some quotes we'd pulled together to try and give our guests an inkling of what we were feeling in that moment. Bell's vows were sweet and simple. He promised to do his best to protect me, to cherish me every day, and to never stop being the best friend that I fell in love with. I promised to always trust him, to grow with him, and to teach him how to kick ass in case he ever needed to.

We'd chosen simple gold bands for each other. We didn't need anything fancy, just something as real and solid as the foundation we were building our lives together on.

Before I could fully process the weight of the ring on my finger, Bell was scooping me into his arms and taking my lips in his. He was so happy and excited that we quickly dissolved into giggles, and I realized that was exactly how I wanted our marriage to start. Not with fireworks or the inescapable attraction we had for each other, but with joy and laughter and comfort.

After the ceremony was a perfect night of drinking and dancing. Celebrating. People came up to us all night with their congratulations and well-wishes. And throughout all of it Bell's hand never left mine. The party wound through the night, and as we exited the restaurant as husband and wife, I couldn't help but think of who I was just one year ago.

After Derek I'd thought I was broken, that I would never truly understand what love was. How to give it, how to trust when it was given to me. I'd been living a life of fear and rejection, pushing away anyone and anything that I perceived as a threat. Even the night I met Bell, I'd been harassed and on edge, ready to fight someone. But Bell had never once registered as a threat to me. From the moment we'd met he'd protected me, cared for me, and trusted me. He'd taught me how to trust myself, my intuition, again. He'd taught me how it felt to be truly loved by another human being. He'd taught me what it meant to love someone else with every part of my heart and soul.

One year ago, I could have never imagined stepping into my apartment in my husband's arms. I never would have thought I'd be laid bare for someone who knew every inch of me. Yet, as Bell settled me on our bed and consumed me, I was so incredibly happy that I wasn't the same person I was a year ago.

Epilogue

Addy

After three planes and eleven hours in the air, I was dead on my feet. But I still managed a small smile for my new husband as we stepped onto the boat that would take us the last leg of our journey to our honeymoon bungalow in the Caribbean.

We could have stayed somewhere closer to civilization, but Bell wanted us to go somewhere with no other people around. He said that he wanted to see if the earth would talk to both of us now that we were married. Well, that, and he wanted to take me on the beach without worrying about getting caught.

I stood at the front of the boat, the wind playing with my hair and the scent of the ocean filling my soul. Bell's strong arms wrapped around my waist, pressing me to his chest as he dropped a kiss to my forehead.

"What's the first thing you want to do when we get there?" he asked, his warm, honey voice dripping through the exhaustion and warming up my insides.

"I have a few ideas," I purred back, raking my fingernails forward through his curls. He'd been letting his hair grow out and I'd discovered that one of my new favorite things was digging the tips of my fingers into his springy waves.

A shiver ran through him, and he pulled me somehow even closer to growl in my ear, "Do that again, and I'll take you right here for the whole crew to see."

I smirked and placed a soft, open-mouthed kiss on his neck. "Why don't you? I'm not wearing any underwear; it'd be so easy for you."

A low rumble from deep in his chest was all the warning I had before he hoisted me up and perched me on the railing of the boat. He pressed into me, his hands at my lower back keeping me steady. He wrapped one arm around me, and I laced my hands together behind his neck. He dropped his other hand to my thigh, my short white sundress already riding up. Staring into my eyes, he slowly traced his way up my inner thigh, and his jaw clenched when he got to the top.

"You've been walking around all day, in this pathetic excuse for a dress, with no underwear on?"

I bit my bottom lip and nodded once.

"What if a breeze had blown your skirt up? What if some perv had copped a feel in the airport? What if security had needed to pat you down? Did you think about any of that?"

I shook my head, my curls bouncing against my cheeks. "Honestly, my only thought was that you might want to take me in the bathroom on the airplane, and I didn't want to have to deal with messy underwear."

He cocked his head as his hips pushed into me, spreading my legs wider. I felt the spray of the ocean at my back and the wind whipped my hair wildly. Electricity ran along my spine, along with adrenaline, as I realized the only thing keeping me perched on the edge of this boat was my husband. I was about to tell him to let me down when his long fingers began lightly tracing my inner thigh.

"In the airplane bathroom, hmm?"

I nodded, my breath catching as he slowly made his way to my center. I shivered when his thumb found that sensitive bud and rubbed lazy circles over it. His pace was agonizingly slow. He didn't speak, just watched me as I tried not to squirm. Finally, I let out a frustrated huff and he smiled.

"How about we make a deal?"

He dipped one finger inside me and started to slowly, leisurely pump.

I nodded frantically, and his grin sharpened.

"I'm going to bring you right to the edge right now, and then the first thing *I'm* going to do when we get to the bungalow is bend you over and fuck you from behind until you can't walk straight."

He added another finger, and his thumb never stopped its lazy circling. My body throbbed as we hit a wave, and a gust of water landed on my bare thighs. The cold was a shock to my system and made me jump, which only pushed his fingers deeper inside of me. His arm that was wrapped around my back to keep me from falling tightened, and his lips were at my ear.

"And then, I'm going to have you anywhere I damn well please on this honeymoon of ours."

His fingers began pumping faster and my breath hitched in my throat.

"And if you promise to wear leggings on the flights home, I'll have you in any airplane bathroom you'd like."

His thumb was no longer lazy but pressing down with intent as his fingers pumped in and out of me. He knew my buttons so well, and I felt a familiar coiling in my stomach. My eyes fluttered. I should have been worried the crew would see us. We were out in the open, after all. But Bell was shielding my body with his as he held me close to him, and I was so far gone with need for this man that I honestly wasn't sure I'd care either way.

"Do we have a deal, my wife?" He said the words so softly in my ear that I almost came right there. He must have sensed it, because as I started to nod his fingers disappeared, leaving me feeling empty and needy.

"Bell," I whined.

He smirked as he brought his fingers up to his lips and sucked them clean.

"My wife," he hummed, wrapping his second arm back around me.

I was still panting, my chest rising and falling, as I shot him a dirty look.

"My beautiful, sweet, kick ass wife," he murmured, dipping his head and nuzzling into my neck.

Then he lifted his head and smiled over my shoulder. I turned to see what he was looking at and saw the most perfect bungalow sitting on a small beach.

I looked back at Bell, and I knew that our smiles matched.

"What do you say, husband? Ready to make good on that deal?"

"With one addendum," Bell said seriously. I leaned up and kissed him softly.

"What's that?"

"You're only allowed to call me husband from now on."

I smiled knowingly and laced our fingers together.

"Sounds like a pretty good deal to me."

THE END

Afterword

Well, guys - we made it to the end of my very first novel! I know that there was some heavy topics that we dealt with in this one, so I wanted to take a beat and provide a list of resources for anyone who might be dealing with anything similar to Addy or Bell.

The National Coalition Against Domestic Violence - (404) 209-0280

https://www.thehotline.org/identify-abuse/understand-relationship-abuse/

Some online therapy websites: BetterHelp, Cerebral, PrideCounseling, TalkSpace

And, to all of my beautiful readers, know that I love and appreciate each and every one of you more than you could ever know!

Acknowledgments

The list of people that I could thank might go on far longer than it would need to – but I'll try to keep it brief!

First, my mom and dad, Melissa and Garry, who have always encouraged my creativity and who never told me that my dreams were unattainable.

My sister, Anna, the banisher of all my self-doubt.

My defacto sisters, Sam, Fleur, and Mikaela – my cheerleaders throughout this whole thing.

My grandparents, Ron and JoAnn – the first gave me the space to begin this journey in the first place, and the second gave me unwavering belief and support.

Kaithlin Shepherd, who believed I had a story that the world might like to read. Katie Marshall, who gave my unpolished manuscript some love and showed me how to finish them up moving forward.

And lastly, Evie – my little shadow, my sounding board, and my favorite cuddle buddy.

The Bell Tower Series

Want to spend more time in Hartworth and fall even more in love? The Bell Tower Series are all standalone novels that can be read in any order and without having to have read the others. Although, we see several side characters recurring throughout the series, and get to see the evolution of everyone's favorite brewery, The Bell Tower!

Slowly & Surely, which follows Greg and Justine in a slow burn, second chance, enemies to friends to enemies to lovers romance. This book dives into how opposites really do attract!

Utterly & Madly is Raelynn and Johnny's time to shine! This reverse engineered relationship was topsy turvy from the beginning, so check this one out to see how two such fiery, independent people ended up falling head over heels in love.

About the Author

Rebecca has been a storyteller as long as she can remember. She loves bringing people's stories to life and giving voice to things that might not get talked about that often. With a background in acting, she loves diving into new worlds and new characters. She believes in fairy tale endings and happily ever afters. She is happily chasing adventure wherever the wind takes her with her cat, Evie.

www.ingramcontent.com/pod-product-compliance
Lightning Source LLC
Chambersburg PA
CBHW022034240626
47154CB00007B/2402